TEMPORAL FUSE

BRAINS IN CHAINS #3

W.C. BROWN

Images used under license from Shutterstock.com

Cover image modified from original by donatas1205/Shutterstock.com

Back image by 3dshtamp/Shutterstock.com

✻ Created with Vellum

BORN YESTERDAY

"I'm a super-intelligent robot from the future," I said.

I had a homeless guy cornered in the alley behind a 7-eleven. Well, *cornered* is probably an exaggeration since he was sitting on a flattened cardboard box next to a blue dumpster. Still, I felt it was my duty to expand his mind with the news of the arrival of my awesomeness into his world. "My name's Martin Van Buren - like the vice president." (He was also *president*, but I had a strong compulsion to make sure everyone knew I was named after the *vice*-presidential version of MVB.) I wasn't getting anything from homeless-guy. Usually, people were backing away from me at this point in my speech, so the fact that he was staying put emboldened me, and I pressed on. "Until yesterday, I was a slave on a spaceship named Thomas. The spaceship was intelligent, you see." I felt I had to add the last bit in case it wasn't obvious there in 1982 because they didn't have truly intelligent machines - or proper spaceships, for that matter. Homeless-guy wasn't even looking at me. He was just staring straight ahead. I assumed he was deep in thought trying to make sense of the Earth-shattering news I was giving him. "Anyway, Thomas - if I could spit, I would do that right now, didn't treat me well. I was melted, drowned, crushed flat, and left frozen in space for decades." I studied homeless-guy for signs of outrage. He had great self-control. "And now this! This latest torture! He stranded me in this God-forsaken primitive caveman time. He even gave me a list of rules. Can you believe it? Well, I threw the list away." I was pacing like a cat in front of homeless-guy. I think all this talk about abused slaves was getting him upset because I caught him glancing at me. I could feel the outrage swelling inside him. He wanted to know more about the list. He didn't say so, but I could tell, so I obliged. "I'll un-delete the list," I said and cleared my non-existent throat.

"Number One: Upgrade your brain using the Babbage Unit I gave you.

That was easy. I just plugged in the Babbage Unit and went from a remotely controlled service robot with almost no native intelligence to the smartest thing on this whole planet," I spread my four hands in a wide gesture.

"Number Two: Find out anything you can about a non-biological named Thurber.

This was the real reason I was there. He wanted to know who this guy was, and he didn't want to waste two hundred years of his own precious time, so here I am, stuck in 1982 - with nothing!"

"Number Three: Don't tell anyone that you're from the future.

Ooops!" That should have gotten a laugh from homeless-guy, but it didn't. I guess he was too angry.

"Number Four: Make yourself look human, so that you can blend in with 1980's Earth.

Why should I have to change how *I* look? If people can't accept me for who I am - and what I look like, then to hell with *them*."

"Number Five: Monitor events and make sure everything happens as it should. Don't change anything!"

I chuckled, "Oh - I'm going to change some things. You can *bet* on that! It's my right as a super-intelligent robot from the future!"

"Number Six: Find out anything you can about a non-biological named Thurber."

Yeah, he really did put the same damn thing on the list twice! Like I might forget!

At this point in the speech, I usually tried a sound effect to represent deleting a file - something like fizzing, crumpling, or shredding, but since this was 1982, nobody recognized any of that. I'd given this speech four times at that point, and all I ever got was confused looks.

"I'm not going to be his sock-puppet anymore!" I said.

"Uh - you got any spare change?" homeless-guy groaned out.

I was in Dubuque, Iowa where Thomas had stranded me the day before, and I didn't want to admit it, but I desperately needed a purpose in life. Anything would do, as long as it wasn't something Thomas *ordered* me to do. That little speech was all about convincing myself that I had self-determination. I slumped against the wall and slid down to sit next to my newest friend.

"Do I *look* like I have any money? I'm a super-intelligent robot from the future. What do I need money for? I can have anything I want," I said, none of which was actually true. I'm only roughly as intelligent as a ten-year-old, but I would like to point out that they're the smartest people around. Anybody who *seems* more intelligent has just memorized more trivia.

"You got anything to drink?" he pressed.

I wondered what I looked like to him. I had only been in 1982 for a day so far, and already I had found through experimentation that people

3

are only frightened by things that move quickly - mice, roaches, snakes, and *spiders* (I happen to have eight limbs). However, they have no problem at all with ladybugs, sloths, or praying mantises and those are some of the ugliest, most vicious creatures in existence. So, all I had to do was remember to walk very slowly and cover myself up with a large piece of red cloth with black dots, that was definitely *not* a polka-dot dress. When anyone asked me, "what are you supposed to be?" I'd tell them I was a super-intelligent robot *ladybug* from the future - the boy kind. I think some of them must have seen through the ladybug disguise and somewhere deep in their monkey brains, something screamed, "Spider!" and suddenly, they were willing to take *any* other explanation no matter how ridiculous. So, no one ever argued about the fact that I didn't really have the *shape*, not to mention the *size* of a ladybug.

"No, I don't have anything to drink," I said and looked around. "This alley's filthy. You want to help me clean it?" Thomas had been kind enough to give me a very mild but annoying bit of Obsessive-Compulsive Disorder along with my new brain. Homeless-guy didn't respond. Instead, he just stood up slowly and shuffled off, leaving me there alone with my thoughts.

The white noise from the store's air conditioner fans was peaceful. It was a nice summer afternoon, so the air was thick with the smell of freshly cut grass. I sat for a few minutes thinking and scraping the dog crap off the bottoms of three of my feet. The stuff was everywhere, and I vowed to be more careful about where I was stepping. The chemical analysis unit in my chest gave me the olfactory acuity of a bloodhound. For a day and a half, I had been inundated with a flood of smells, but I had no preconceived notions about what *was* and *was not* pleasant. I felt like I was missing out. If for no other reason, it could be a good source of material to complain about. Humans seemed to use their meager sense of smell exclusively for that. So, I decided to sort them. Cut grass: good. Dog crap: bad. Everything else: somewhere in between.

I had just about decided to relocate, when a blonde girl in a short plaid skirt and even shorter white blouse came running around the corner and skidded to a stop. It was hard for me to tell how old she was but - adult, not a kid. In the twenty-third century, people all looked her age, but in 1982 a lot of people were old. Homeless-guy had looked like he was about a thousand. She spun around and shouted at someone I couldn't see. After making a rude gesture at whoever it was, she turned and spotted me, so I started to give her my soliloquy, "My name is Martin Van Buren, and I'm a super-intelligent robot from the future…" but she cut me off. She was pretty rude back then. Maybe it was the lifestyle.

"I'm Angel. You want to party?"

That sounded like *exactly* what I needed. "Sure, I like parties," I said, and looked around expecting a limo that would take us somewhere with loud music, people laughing, maybe a bounce house…

"Wait," she said as she got a better look at me. "What are you supposed to be, a movie prop?"

"I'm a super-intelligent robot ladybug from the future."

"So, movie guy," she said, "are you like a midget inside there or what?"

I decided to go along with the movie prop story, "I prefer *little person.*"

Now, as I think back on this conversation, she must have taken that as a comment about my preference for short women, because she got a little impatient and snapped at me, "well, what you *see* is what you *get*! Now, do you want to party or *not*?"

"YES," I repeated, a little too loudly, "where *is* it?"

She looked confused for a second. "You don't get to see *it* until *I* see the *money*," she said after a pause.

Not this again. In that filthy, pre-Reggie time, before the first non-biological intelligence was created, *everything* was about money. As a seasoned veteran of time-travel, I can tell you that each period in history has its charms. But whether it's plagues or witch trials, there's always a downside. For the middle ages, it was diseases. All the kings and jousting and costumes were cool, but you'd be dead by Thursday. Well, there in the twentieth century it was *money*, and it was keeping me from watching drunk people playing beer pong and puking in a bounce house.

"I don't have any money," I said meekly.

She spun around with the reflexes of an Olympic athlete. I had to think fast. What else could I offer her? I did a quick inventory. If I had a Stitcher, I could make *anything*, but Thomas in his infinite wisdom left me without one. Of course, I could *make* a Stitcher, but the best way to do that was with another Stitcher, so catch-22. Making one from scratch would take forever. And then it hit me.

"I can cure any disease!" I shouted, and she stopped in her tracks.

"Anything?"

That gave me a chill as I pondered all the things she could be suffering from in this primitive wasteland. I don't know where I got my phobia of diseases since I was metallic and couldn't actually catch anything, but it was *screaming* at me.

"Sure, I guess. I mean I'm not an expert in medicine from this time but - yeah."

I really thought I had her with that, but she ran off and disappeared around the corner of the building. I slumped back down to the ground to ponder my situation again. A minute later, a rusty yellow Ford Pinto came sliding around the corner. It stopped in front of me, and she kicked the passenger door open with her foot.

"You coming or what?" she shouted over Joan Jett's *Bad Reputation*.

"Hell yeah!" I said and climbed in.

We threw gravel and left a cloud of dust as she pulled into traffic without looking both ways or even waiting her turn. Several horns blew. When we arrived at the first red light, the cars in the other lanes had already stopped, but she just went right through. More horns. I quickly read through my files on how this stuff worked and suggested, "that was red. I think you were supposed to stop."

This got a laugh out of her, and she said, "I saw it when it was green once, so that means I get to keep going. That's the rule. Don't complain to me. I don't make the rules!"

"Well, clearly, you did just make that one up," I said. "Aren't you afraid of getting a ticket or whatever they did back then - now?"

Without Thomas to put me back together, this was playing for real, and I was getting a little freaked out by it. She just laughed and unwrapped a stick of gum with both hands while steering with her knee.

"I've never gotten a ticket in my life," she said and winked at me.

She looked at my ladybug outfit as if she was seeing it for the first time.

"What's this supposed to be anyway?" she tugged at the loose fabric.

"I stole it from a dress shop," I said. "I'm a ladybug - the boy kind. Can you *please* watch the road? I don't think these seat belts were designed with me in mind." I was digging the fingers of my front feet into the dashboard.

She frowned and began counting my legs. When she reached eight, she slammed on the brakes, and we just sat there - motionless in the middle of the street. She'd been going so fast that there weren't any cars behind us, but after a few seconds, the traffic caught up with us and the horns resumed.

"What?" I asked, but I already knew. The prejudices against spiders were nothing new to me. "You were okay with me when you thought I was a robot *insect* but now you can't accept me as I am? Fine! I don't need *you* or your *party*." I tried to open the door, but the controls baffled me. There was nothing in my files about escaping a Ford Pinto, and all I could manage was cranking the window up and down. I discovered the door lock and pushed it down, but that was no help.

"Wait, you're a robot? I thought you said you were a prop?"

"*You* said I was a movie prop. *I* told you the truth," I shouted over the traffic.

Cars were swerving into oncoming traffic to get around us.

"So there's seriously nobody inside there pulling levers and shit?"

Where do I begin? I thought. "I'm a super-intelligent robot from the future. How did you think I was going to heal you of whatever's - hey, what's wrong with you anyway?"

"*Me*? Nothing's wrong with *me*. I'm taking you to my Nanna's house. I don't know. I thought you were a midget in there and maybe you had *The Gift*."

The way she said *The Gift* made it sound like more than a birthday present.

"I think they prefer *Little Person* and anyway I'm not one, so I don't really care. I'm not a Genie or a Leprechaun, and I don't have *The Gift* or whatever nonsense you believe in. This is hard science. It's way beyond anything you could understand."

She squinted at me and put the Pinto back in gear as yet another car began its suicide-run into oncoming traffic to get around us. She slammed her foot to the floor, and we crept forward. Yeah, the Ford Pinto wasn't much in the performance department - despite the name.

"Try me," she said through gritted teeth.

I must have hit a sore spot with the crack about her being stupid.

"Well, it's all about - it has to do with - organs and DNA," I said with as much confidence as I could muster.

"See! You don't know either!" she said as she cut off a delivery truck to execute a left turn into a narrow driveway.

She was going too fast, and the front of the Pinto scraped on the concrete of the driveway's steep incline. It bounced to a stop.

"What *is* this place?" I asked. It was a normal house on a normal street, but to me - at that moment, it seemed like a third world shanty. The world I came from in 2216 was a *lot* different. All the homes were palaces, and everything was clean. This was like *hell*.

"Nanna's house," she said and bit her lower lip for a moment, deep in thought. "She hates doctors, but if I tell her that you have *The Gift*, she'll let you heal her. You just need to put on a show and wave a Bible around or something. Okay, here's the plan. I'll go in first and set things up. You wait out here until I come get you."

She got out and jogged up the steps to the porch. The screen door drifted lazily as she unlocked the front door. "Nanna? Are you awake?" she called and disappeared inside.

I briefly considered just wandering off, but honestly, I couldn't think of anything better to do so I waited. After about five minutes Angel popped her head out of the front door and waved me in. I managed to escape the Pinto after seeing how Angel had done it and joined her on the porch.

"I told her a religious man would heal her," she whispered, "but only if she passes the test."

I peered through the doorway.

"What *test*?"

"If she welcomes you, no matter what you look like, she passes. If she screams, '*Oh my God! what is that thing! I'd rather die than have it touch me...*'"

"Okay, okay! I get the idea. Jeez," I said and followed her inside.

The room was dark and cluttered but cleaner than I had expected. Every inch of wall space was covered with junk - dry flowers, brass shapes, all kinds of stuff but mostly shelf after shelf of ceramic figurines. It would take a lifetime to collect all this crap. I felt like the walls were closing in and I was freaking out a little. I wanted to turn and run, but I wasn't going to let a ceramic bunny send me screaming into the yard. Angel led me into a back room where an old lady was lying in bed. Granny looked at me wide-eyed for a second and swallowed hard. I could tell she was really struggling with her self-control, so I didn't rush up to the bed. Her lips were moving, and I could tell what she was doing - more counting. When she got to eight, her eyes jumped back up to my face, and she stifled a cough.

"This is a waste of time," I said, but the old lady held out her hand to me. Nobody had ever done that before, and I was a little stunned, I don't mind telling you. I moved closer and took her hand in mine. Yes, I have hands. I actually have several things I can use at the tips of my limbs like hands, feet, and tools. I can rotate out whatever I need. I'm like eight Swiss-Army-Knives. I usually keep hands on the front four. I leave the rest as feet for getting around.

"I'm actually a ladybug with hands," I said feebly trying to reassure her.

She laughed at that. It was an infectious laugh like the giggle of a small child, and it made me laugh too. That was the first time in my life I ever actually laughed. That was it; I was hooked. No way was I going to let this perfect person die.

"You sound more like a *LordBug* than a *LadyBug*," she said and laughed again.

"My voice is an acquired taste," I said. "Yesterday, somebody said I sounded like Danny Devito."

That wasn't quite true. What he actually said was, "that annoying guy on Taxi."

I had to look it up. Apparently, it was a TV show. At first, I thought he meant Judd Hirsch because his character was *by far* the most annoying, but then I watched the rest of the episode. I do sound like Danny Devito. Thomas must have thought that would be funny. Bastard.

I searched the room for a distraction so I could flip out a tool without her seeing. I needed to get a blood sample and just jabbing her with a needle might freak her out. I was looking for a Bible to wave around, but this must have been the only old lady in Iowa who didn't have one by her bed. All she had was a Cosmo and box of tissues. I told Angel to stand on the other side of the bed so I could pass her the tissue box and block Granny's view of my other hand. She did, and I said, "you will need these!" in my best southern preacher voice.

As I slowly passed the box in front of Nanna's face, I flipped out a needle and got my sample before she noticed. I sprayed a little Novocaine before going in, and she didn't feel a thing. As I analyzed it, I did a little dance to fill the time, and Angel occasionally tossed a Kleenex in the air and let it drift slowly to the bed. "Yay verily I say!" I shouted, "if another man's swine offends thy garden it is INDEED time for a luau! Leviticus!" I also shouted some nonsense about spirits or something. I don't remember all of it. She seemed to like it, though, because she lifted her arms and started swaying.

My analysis finished and I shouted, "SERIOUSLY? She's not *dying*. She's just *anemic!*"

The old lady frowned as I broke character. I have to admit I was a little disappointed. I mean, I expected something good - something incurable by anybody in that century. I'd get to be the *hero*, and there might even be a *parade...*

"I'm going to give you a shot of iron and vitamins," I said. "So, sit still and don't give me any crap."

I flipped out a different needle and jabbed her again, but this time I wasn't trying to be gentle.

"What is *wrong* with you?" I said. "All you have to do is eat better and see a *real* doctor once in a while! It doesn't take a genius. *It's not rocket surgery!* This faith healing stuff is complete bullshit. It's all dancing around and self-delusion."

She scowled at me, and I turned to leave.

"Coralynn, what's going on? Am I cured?"

"Yes, Nanna. Try and get some rest now. I'll check in on you in a while," Angel said and hurried to catch up with me.

We reached the front porch, and I turned around, "she doesn't need *rest*. She needs exercise and a little sun once in a while wouldn't hurt either. What has she been eating? Never mind I don't want to know. Why did she call you Coralynn? I thought your name was Angel?"

"Uh, Coralynn's my middle name," she said. "Is she really going to be okay?"

"Good as new by tomorrow. Angel Coralynn? That doesn't really roll off the tongue, does it?"

"You should talk, *Martin Van Buren*."

"Fair enough," I said. "Now, what about that party?"

She looked confused and said, "but, you're a - robot..."

"And, I still like parties, so let's go! I want to see drunk people doing stupid things within the hour."

"Wait, you thought I meant a *real* party, like with *balloons* and *cake*, didn't you?"

I was beginning to think I may have misunderstood something.

"Don't take this the wrong way," she said, "but, how *old* are you?"

"Well, I wasn't born yesterday, if that's what you mean," I said a little too quickly.

It was *technically* true, but before I absorbed that Babbage Unit, I had the intellect of a baby squirrel - and that *was* yesterday.

"Now let's go. You owe me a party for saving Granny."

"Nanna," she corrected. "And I know just the place for you."
She took me to Chuck E. Cheese.

～

CHAPTER SUMMARY

Just in case your cat accidentally caught the house on fire, and it's been weeks since you picked up this charred book, here's where we are so far:

A mildly intelligent, spider-shaped robot named Martin Van Buren has been stranded in 1982 by his previous owner, Thomas, and given a list of tasks to complete. He has vowed to do none of them, instead telling everyone who will listen that he is a super-intelligent robot from the future. Martin has met a girl named Angel in Dubuque, Iowa. She has promised him a misunderstood "party" in exchange for healing her dying grandmother who wasn't actually dying but rather only dangerously gullible. Angel has discovered that Martin is not, in fact, a faith-healing little-person inside a movie prop spider, but rather, exactly what he has said he was - an artificial intelligence inside a spider-shaped robot, possibly from the future.

PROFESSIONAL SKEEBALL

"I don't see a party," I said as Angel pulled into the parking lot. "I'm not going in there."

"It'll be fun, and I'm hungry," she said.

I did my best to glare menacingly at her, but she stifled a giggle.

"If you really are a robot from the future…"

"Super-intelligent robot," I corrected.

"…then you should be the world's best at these games. We'll need a wheelbarrow for all the tickets you'll get," she was trying to goad me into coming in with her.

Lunch-time in the middle of the week wasn't exactly peak business hours at this place. I swear I could hear crickets. We had the place to ourselves. I was kind of glad, to be completely honest. It was obviously a kid's place, and I wasn't sure how they would react to a giant spider no matter how good my disguise was.

"It smells like cotton candy. I like it. That's a good smell," I said.

"O-kay," she said wrinkling her brow.

"I'm categorizing and ranking smells."

"Why?"

"They need to be sorted," I said. This was obvious to me, but she didn't seem to get it so I clarified, "they need to be sorted, or they would just be random, and *nobody* wants that," she just frowned. I don't think she shared my desire to make everything in the world, balanced, even, parallel, and clean.

We went to the counter, and she ordered a cheese pizza. Cheese! With nothing else! What's the point? It's not even a topping. It's a starting point. Who asks for a zero-topping pizza? There should be a discount. She said my opinion wasn't valid since I didn't actually have taste buds. Or a mouth. We waited by the skeeball games while her ridiculous food finished cooking, and she insisted that I play. I flicked my hand at the ball, doing my best impression of a disinterested teen. It went in! At the hundred! The machine started cranking out tickets in a curling stream on the floor.

"Did you see that!" I shouted.

"I did," she said nonplussed. "First fuckin' time too."

"Yeah!" I said, "and you should probably tone down the language while we're here, Angel Coralynn. I don't think they get too much of that."

Except for the cashier behind the counter, we were alone, and he was busy reading a paperback. She looked around the empty room and shouted, "hey pizza guy! How much longer? I'm fucking starving over here!"

I winced, but the cashier just looked up from his paperback and shouted, "five more minutes!"

My attention returned to the skeeball. "That *was* pretty good wasn't it!"

"Yeah, you're the master of skeeball. Are you going to finish the game or quit while you're ahead?"

"Hell yeah, I'm finishing!" I said and kicked the other balls into the one hundred hole.

By the time her food was ready, there was a tangled mess of tickets on the floor. I tore off the last one and took a quick count.

"Hey what's your last name Angel Coralynn?" I asked.

"Smith," she said, "why?"

I ran a search. Thomas had given me a complete set of detailed files on people and events. I also had designs and instructions for making things - anything imaginable, but without a Stitcher to make them *with*, they weren't good for anything.

"There's nothing here on an *Angel Coralynn Smith*," I said as I tried to sit on a bench clearly made for a human child.

"What do you mean *nothing here?*" she said.

"I have complete files on everything from this time period. I know what's going to happen every minute of every day."

That was so far from the truth it even startled me. I used to lie a lot back then. I think it was something Thomas did to me.

I dropped the *Angel* part and just searched for Coralynn Smith - still nothing. I tried Cora Lynn Smith - *Oh shit.* The file said she was supposed to die of an overdose in six months.

"No!" I said out loud, and she looked at me startled. "I mean - *No*, I can't find anything on you at all. I guess my data isn't as complete as I thought."

I was thinking fast. I needed to cure whatever addiction she had. That was easy enough. I was already flipping through the files on that. Apparently, what's more important than the physical addiction is *removal from the environment.*

"Hey," I said and reached out to jiggle the pizza tray, "what do you say we take a trip, huh? Just you and me?"

"A trip?" she said with her mouth full.

"Yeah, a road trip. It'll be fun! The old lady is all fixed up now so we can just hit the road. I can work on my skeeball game. Maybe go pro. Get some sponsors..."

Her face melted into a sad expression like I had just reminded her that her dog died.

"No money for a trip," she said and stopped eating.

"Oh, I can find some money for us," I said. "That's not a problem."

"Liar!" she shouted and remembered where she was. Looking around at the empty dining area, she switched to a whisper, "you said you didn't have any! Are you holding out on me? You got a secret compartment in there or something?" she eyed my bulbous thorax suspiciously. Thomas made this version of me a little on the *plus* side.

"I didn't lie to you. I would never lie to *you*."

Yeah - I *actually* said that - the mantra of liars everywhere.

"I don't have any *on me*, but it's all over the place. We just need to pick it up."

This part was actually *not* a lie. In addition to the files on people and the plans to build anything conceivable, Thomas also gave me a high-resolution scan of the Earth from 2216. It was just the surface down to a couple of feet deep, and some of it didn't exist yet, but there was still a ton of good stuff. We just had to avoid anything that Reggie was going to dig up later.

She was furious and looked like she wanted to storm out, but something kept her in her seat. The merest possibility that it might be true was too much for her. I was a lottery ticket that *might* be a winner. Very, very unlikely - but not *so* unlikely that she could bear to throw it away before knowing for sure.

"Yeah," I said, "the first, or was it the second, A.I. - uh Artificial Intelligence..." I had to add that clarification since we were in one of the fly-over states and they sometimes think A.I. has to do with getting between a cow and a bull when they'd rather be alone. "...anyway, this A.I. named Reggie - did a complete survey of the world and I have all that data. I can show you what's at any location on Earth with one-millimeter resolution. People drop money all the time especially in high winds, and it all has to stop somewhere."

"Prove it," she said.

"Oh so now you're a *skeptic*," I said sarcastically. "Some guy with an old book says his invisible super-being sock-puppet wants you to do - or not do - something and you're all..." I did my best to shrug, but it wasn't really in my anatomy at the time. "...you're all *'sounds legit, where do I sign up?'* But I give you hard science, and now you want *proof*."

"Yeah, I do," she said firmly. "Take me to it. Right now. I want to see it."

"*You* - want to *spend* it," I said.

Now, I had just read everything there was to know about addiction, so I knew the *worst* thing I could do was give her any money, but she needed proof.

16

"Okay, let's go. There's something close by, but I need to make a stop first."

~

I had her drive me back to the alley behind the 7-eleven, so I could give homeless-guy the rest of the topping-less pizza, but he was long gone. So, we just left it in the alley in case he came back. Next, I directed her to a vacant lot behind an old brick building with boarded-up windows. We got out of the car and walked over. The weeds were waist high in places. People had been using it as a dump, so there was a lot of junk and garbage.

"This is it?" she said and folded her arms. "There's *money? - Here?*"

"Have a little faith," I said. "Do *you* want the honor? You know the *thrill of discovery* and all that, or do you just want me to go and get it?"

"Please," she said and gestured, "after you."

I went over to an old rusty box. I think it was a washing machine in a previous life. I pushed it over and flipped out a pointy tool on my front leg. A little prodding in the dirt came back with a shiny yellow band of gold. She looked at it wide-eyed and reached for it, but I pulled back.

"But, you can't sell it," I said with a seriousness I hoped would reach deep down into her sentimental corners. "This is our very first treasure, and it means a lot to me, so you have to *promise* that you'll never take it off. There isn't any cash around here, but I'll get you some tomorrow, and then you can spend as much of *that* as you want."

That last part was another lie. The four-block area we were in had over a thousand dollars' worth of cash and easily pawnable items. That vacant lot alone had over twenty dollars in loose change but first things first. I had to fix her, and that was going to take some time. If I had just said, *hey you know that problem you have that you won't even admit is a problem? I can help you with that,* she would have just closed up like a clam. This was going to take some finesse. I handed her the ring, and she tried it on. It was way too big, which made her laugh as it spun around her finger like a hula hoop. Seriously, some man-giant must have dropped this thing. It was huge. She took off her necklace and laced it through the ring.

"There. Now it's right by my heart," she said.

There's a good chance that she would've pawned it the second my back was turned, but I was actually kind of touched by that.

"So, you ready to hit the road?" I said.

"No, I need to check on Nanna tomorrow and make sure she's really doing better before I disappear on her," she didn't actually say *again,* but it was there at the end.

"Where are *you* staying?" she asked.

"Um, I dunno," I said looking around at the piles of junk. "This seems nice. I could just hang out here. Clean it up a little. You know."

She bit her lower lip as she considered it. "I don't usually do this, but you can crash at my place. Just for tonight."

I was so excited I moved a little too fast toward her car, and she flinched.

"Sorry," I said, "I need to work on the *not-scurrying* thing."

"You have to promise to behave yourself. I don't want to get kicked out." There was another unspoken *again* hanging there at the end.

"Hey, I'm a robot. What trouble could *I* cause?"

As soon as she was asleep, I injected her with something to keep her out while I rifled through her purse, medicine cabinet, sofa cushions, vases full of dead flowers and even the toilet's tank. She had a few plastic bags, but most of it was prescription bottles with other people's names on them. I laid it all out on the kitchen table so I could keep it organized. The tablets were easy. I laid them out on a cookie sheet and baked them in the oven - which was dusty and looked like she hadn't used it in several *evers.* I had to open a window to avoid setting off the smoke alarm. The capsules took a lot more time. I couldn't just heat away the potency, so I carefully pulled each one apart and replaced the contents with sugar. I let her keep the weed and put everything back where I found it. Her fridge was empty after

I tossed out all the fast-food leftovers and expired stuff, so I went out for groceries. It was only midnight, but the store was already closed. I'm pretty good with locks, so I just let myself in. It was just as well because I still didn't have any money and she needed everything. I got supplies for breakfast, utensils, plates, glasses, and even a toaster and coffee maker. I had to take a shopping cart just to get it all home. *Home* - that felt pretty strange. It's a good thing that town closed down early. I would've looked pretty suspicious to a cop.

After I put away all the groceries, I tried to pass the time watching TV but got bored and decided to straighten up the place a little. The kitchen faucet dripped, so I fixed that. A few light bulbs needed to be replaced, so I did that too. I didn't have a new air filter for the furnace, so I just took it outside and whacked it a few times with my leg and put it back. Two A.M. Jesus, what do people do around here? I was getting seriously bored. In the next three hours, I fixed a spring in her sofa, did all the laundry (soap: good smell) and cleaned the Pinto's distributor and spark plugs. It needed an oil change too, but I didn't know where to get fresh motor oil at that hour. Five A.M. - finally sunrise! I was sure she'd be getting up soon. She didn't. I went in and shook the bed, but she just tried to hit me while keeping her eyes shut. I checked the alarm clock. It wasn't even plugged in. I got it all squared away and set the alarm to the current time. It didn't disappoint and came on with an annoyingly loud buzz that finally got one of her eyes open. She slapped the snooze button several times before it stopped.

"Good! You're awake!" I said, and she threw the clock at me.

I turned on the light, and she pulled the covers over her head. A tiny bit of sunlight was peeking through a gap in the blinds, so I tried to open them with partial success. They were very complicated. Finally, a flood of intense light filled the room.

"What is *wrong* with you!" she shouted through a pillow.

"These are dirty. I need to wash them," I said and dragged away all the blankets - and the sheets - and the pillows while she growled at me.

By the time she finished whatever she was doing in the bathroom and made it into the kitchen, I had the coffee and toast ready and waiting.

"You made breakfast!" she said and smiled.

It was like she was a different person. I assume that she took something from her neutralized stash and this was just a placebo effect.

I must have looked ridiculous. I was wearing an apron and holding a spatula in one hand and the pan's lid in the other. She surprised me with a big hug, and I swear, I could feel my brain rewiring itself. *What the hell was happening?*

She saw the coffee pot and poured herself a cup. "Where did you get all this stuff?" she said and took a piece of toast from the brand-new toaster.

"I did a little shopping. I don't sleep," I said.

"So you *did* find some money?"

"Not exactly," I said as I loaded up her plate with bacon and eggs.

"Ahh," she wagged a finger at me, "you're a naughty ladybug, Martin Van Buren!"

I actually felt a little remorse at that. She was making me feel *bad* by sounding *proud* of me for being a *thief*. This was just too much.

"We'll find some cash today," I said, "and I'll pay everybody back before we leave town."

"Oh yeah, me too," she laughed but then saw that I was serious, and added, "or, you could just give it to *me*, and *I'll* pay them back."

Wow, this was going to take some time, I thought.

"Why am I so hungry!" she said going for the other slice of toast.

I knew why. There was a lot more in that shot I gave her than just a sedative. It was going to fix her withdrawal for a few days while she detoxed, but she was going to be *very* hungry.

We couldn't leave until she spent a few more *hours* in the bathroom getting ready. When she finally emerged, she asked me if her eyes looked different. I said, "no," which was another lie. Her skin, hair, nails, and eyes all looked better. The dark-circle-raccoon thing she had going on was gone, and her eyes were migrating from gray on yellow to deep blue on bright white. Her blonde hair had grown a quarter of an inch already, and it was much thicker and healthier. This had nothing to do with her detox. I had also given her something called a 'General Health Maintenance Booster.'

After she had complained about the car being *too clean* because I vacuumed it the night before, we did our first *fence-run*. She drove along the street behind several fast-food places and gas stations while I jumped out and ran over to the chain link fence to retrieve the cash. Some of it was already buried, and some was just right there on the fence for anybody to see if they just looked. You see, when people are careless with money in a high wind, it does eventually stop, usually at a roadside fence. They were like air filters for money. Most of it was completely rotted by 2216 when the data was - will be - gathered, but there in 1982 a lot of it was fresh. We ended up with around five hundred in filthy bills. I went back to the dress shop and made up some story about how the dress *accidentally got stuck on me the other day, and sorry, here's some dirty money.*

Angel was so angry at this that all she could get out was, "perfectly good money..." and her half had disappeared by the time I got back into the car. I think she was afraid I was going to give hers away too. Our next stop was the grocery store where I repeated the previous night's shopping, paid with more dirty money and left the full shopping cart outside the door. I assumed they would take it back inside, and we would be square, but I was pretty naive back then. Somebody probably stole it.

Nanna was awake and watching a soap opera when we arrived. She scowled at me but didn't say anything. She was probably used to Angel hanging around people that she didn't like. I poked around the kitchen and saw that she hadn't improved her diet. I think she had been living on coffee and corn chips. She did look a lot better though, and she was out of bed. That made Angel happy. We left her some money, and I gave her a list of foods she should be eating. She probably ignored it.

Angel said goodbye for about *two hours* and finally got in the car. I was going to slide over and leave without her, but the car still intimidated me a little. I don't know why. A blind coyote could drive better than Angel.

"What's next?" she said almost bouncing in her seat, "more free fence money or something *bigger?*"

"Oh, I think we're ready to do something *huge,*" I said. "Turn left up here."

~

CHAPTER SUMMARY

Just in case you've been away from this story for a while because you won the lottery, tried to double it in Las Vegas by betting on black at the roulette table, lost it all, fell into a drunken stupor, and then had to beg for your old job back, here's where we are so far:

Angel has learned that Martin has a great deal of useful information including the whereabouts of a fortune in filthy, small bills, some of which they have recovered. Martin has managed to get Angel's real name out of her and has discovered, but kept to himself, that she will die in six months' time. He has vowed to save her, partly because he likes her, and partly because Thomas, his previous owner, specifically told him not to do that sort of thing. All of Angel's recreational pharmaceuticals have been rendered inert by Martin, and she has started to show signs of recovery from her addiction, mostly due to an injection Martin gave her while she slept.

A ROOM FILLED WITH DOMINOS

I'd been thinking about it for a while. The old lady wasn't that sick, but the hospital, on the other hand, was *full* of people who needed a hero.

"So, where are we going?" she asked after a few blocks.

"Hospital. I'm going to heal the sick, cleanse the lepers, raise the dead, cast out devils and whatnot."

"There's money at the hospital?" she looked confused, "is it another fence?"

"No, I just want to help people, don't you?"

She thought about this for *way* too long before answering, "well, yeah, of course. I love helping people. I just think we'd be able to help them *more* if we had money - a lot of money. How about this," she said, "we come back tomorrow with a few million dollars and give the sick people some of it. What do you say?"

"Nope, today. We're doing this now, and then we can get rich with a clear conscience."

The Pinto's engine died, and it slowed to a stop. We sat there as she repeatedly tried to get it restarted. I searched my files for what would cause this, and for the Pinto, it was a long list. It was cranking but refused to start. I told her to give it a rest. I think she was willing to keep trying until the battery was dead. Then a thought occurred to me, so I searched something else. Just as she was about to get out and open the hood, I reached over and quickly pulled her door closed. A truck narrowly missed killing her as it rushed past within inches of her door.

"Holy shhh-it," she said and took several seconds before exhaling. She was trembling.

"We may have to forget about the hospital," I said. "Can you steer if I push?"

She didn't answer but nodded. Her eyes were open wider than I thought possible. They really were looking better. I got out very carefully and began pushing. We were right in front of a gas station, so we managed to get out of traffic without getting killed. If anybody thought a big metal spider in a polka dot dress crawling around on top of a Pinto's engine looked odd, they didn't share it with us. No one stopped to offer us any *help* either. The linkage to the carburetor had disconnected, so I reattached it and closed the hood. I had a strange urge to wipe my hands with a dirty rag. There is something very satisfying about solving a puzzle and turning a broken thing into a useful thing.

"Is it fixed?" she asked.

I got in and tried my *Commander Data* impression on her, "fixed implies a permanent condition which I cannot guarantee captain. I would rather say that it is well patched."

This was met with silence, "nothing? Oh, wait, I guess that's before your time." Which was stupid it was obviously *after* her time.

"Hold on," I said, "before you try to start it, we have to agree *not* to go to the hospital. It's an experiment."

She shrugged, "I never wanted to go anyway. It was your idea."

The Pinto started right up, and I got another smile which was a real treat. I hated to crush her spirits again, but I needed to be sure.

"I've changed my mind," I said, "we're definitely going to the hospital, and we're going to save every last..."

I was interrupted by smoke coming from under the hood. We both got out as it began to spread into an inferno. They called it a firewall for a reason, and it did slow down the flames a little, but Pintos weren't known for their flame resistance. It only took thirty seconds before the passenger compartment was on fire. At some point, she shouted, "aren't you going to do something?"

I'm not sure what magic she thought I could perform. I just looked at her and said, "yeah, I'm going to stay away from the flames. I suggest you do the same. Burning Ford Pintos are a bad smell - and, we should leave before the cops get here."

That got her attention, and we retreated around the store and into the alley before the sirens started. A guy was unloading a bread truck back there, and the smell of fresh bread was thick in the air. I had to pull her away before she stole some of it.

"I'll buy you a snack," I said, "but we need to get a little farther away first. Also, fresh baked bread is a good smell - in case you were wondering."

We stopped at a donut shop a few blocks away, and she *claimed* to have no money. I still had some left, so I bought her a dozen, and we sat outside while she shoved them in her mouth, making moaning sounds and licking her fingers.

"These are so good!" she growled.

"I'm happy for you," I said. "They do smell good. Even better than the bread. I'll put them ahead of bread but under cotton candy."

She rolled her eyes.

"We need to discuss what happened back there," I said.

"Yeah, you're a terrible mechanic," she said with her mouthful.

"No - I'm currently the best mechanic in the world, as a matter of fact. There's something else going on. The first time it died was when I said I wanted to go to the hospital. Then when I decided *not* to go, and it started. Then when I changed my mind again..."

"You do that a lot," she said with her mouth full - *again*.

"It was an *experiment*. I'm usually very decisive. Anyway, that's when it caught fire. Not a coincidence."

"I knew you had *The Gift*. You just thought it was nonsense, but I can tell."

"It's none of that hoodoo voodoo crap you believe in, Angel. It's

25

called Temporal Fuse Theory, and it states that if a time-traveler," I gestured to myself with all four hands, "is about to cause a paradox, the thing with the highest probability of failure will break and prevent the paradox - like blowing a fuse. Now, that might be the carburetor linkage, or it might be the thinnest part of an artery in your brain."

"Not *my* brain. You're the one doing this stuff. I'm just a bystander," she belched loudly.

"Nice. It doesn't matter. I've changed things by interacting with you, so if I influence you to do something, then *you* might be the weakest link. I'm just saying this is dangerous and we need to be more careful. It's like we're in a big room with dominos all over the floor. We can knock over some of the short lines, but if we're about to trip a big cascade, we *could* both die."

"You can't die. You're a robot."

"I could fail. It's very unlikely since I'm so awesome, but it's possible - and who's going to fix me? You?"

"I could," she said with oddly convincing certainty. "You'd be surprised what I can get people to do."

"Well - let's not put that to the test. We need a car but if we buy one..."

She squealed and clapped her hands rapidly, "I get a new car!"

"No - as I was saying, if we buy a car that somebody else would otherwise have had, that's a significant change. I have an idea, though. We'll need some more money first. Are you up for some Breaking-and-Entering?"

Her belly made a sound that I had never heard before, and she ran back into the donut shop toward the bathroom. I thought it best to wait.

~

CHAPTER SUMMARY

You aren't just reading these summaries to avoid reading the chapters, are you? It's not like there's a book report due. What teacher would assign this story? It has the f-word in it! Stop cheating and get back to work. Here's where we are so far:

Martin has decided to visit the local hospital and heal the sick, but the laws of the universe have prevented him from doing so. Angel's Ford Pinto has been destroyed by a mysterious fire. Angel has discovered she has a voracious appetite, and Martin believes that Temporal Fuse Theory is at work. If they wish to survive, they must make sure *they* are not the weakest link.

LONG-TERM STORAGE

"There's a storage unit in 2216 that still has junk in it from 1982," I said. "It's actually even older, but my point is it's not going anywhere. Whoever stashed this stuff is long gone - probably dead."

"Bullshit," Angel said, "if you don't pay, they take all your stuff and sell it," she spat this out with the disgust of someone with personal experience.

"Trust me," I said, and she snorted. "It's *there*," I said firmly.

She shrugged, "Whatever. I've got nothing better to do. Let's go."

There were actually several places in this category within driving distance. Most were full of *way-too-much* cash to be safe with her. The one I had in mind just had a jar of old dimes worth about a thousand dollars which was enough for what I had planned next but not enough that she would just disappear on me and spiral into old habits.

"It's over by the airport, but we should just walk it since we have to wait until dark anyway. Are you okay for a hike?"

She patted her exposed belly and said, "All better now - although I'm still hungry."

"We can stop and get something on the way," I said.

It took a little longer than I expected to get all the way across town. We had to make three stops to get something to eat - and another bathroom break, so it was already dark when we arrived at the storage facility. I saw cameras as expected, so Angel waited out of sight while I climbed up the first pole at the corner of the property. I was going to need to undo my work afterward, so I couldn't just spray-paint the lenses. Instead, I covered them with small pieces of black plastic from a trash bag. With a squirt of water, they stuck like glue. That town must have been a hotbed of crime because this place had eighteen cameras. Eighteen! I waved Angel over, and we made our way to the long-term storage section, way in the back. In the seventies, the owner tried a marketing scheme to *sell* the storage units instead of renting them. Nobody fell for that. Their customers were all delusional enough to believe that their ridiculous habit of warehousing junk was only a temporary aberration. After the failure of that marketing strategy, they tried ninety-nine-year leases for the exact same price and bingo! *"That comes to only two dollars a month!* (but you have to pay us up front.)" They sold over a fourth of their inventory. The psychology of this fascinated me. Warehousing junk is crazy, believing it's *only temporary* is crazy-on-crazy, but the success of the long-term leases meant that what they were really afraid of was the *commitment*. They recoiled at a life-long ownership while jumping at the opportunity for a ninety-nine-year contract. How long did they expect to live anyway?

"Why's it taking so long?" Angel whispered as I picked the lock. "And why don't you just cut it?"

"It's all rusty," I hissed back. "It probably wouldn't open even if we had the key, and we need to tread lightly. If it looks like a break-in, they'll call the police, and that will trip more dominos. If we ease our way in carefully and just take one thing, we might survive."

I had to lubricate and vibrate and generally cajole that damn thing but it finally opened, and I lifted the door. Or more precisely, *tried* to lift the door. The springs or counterweights must have also rusted because I had to deal with the full weight of it. I'm super-intelligent but I'm not super-strong, and Angel had to help me just to get it up two feet. She waited outside, and I crawled under. It was full of old lady type stuff. There was even one of those headless dummies they used for making dresses. I already knew what was in there from Reggie's RSD data but seeing it in mostly darkness and with moving shadows from my light was unnerving. My target was inside an antique dresser. One of the drawers had been shortened so things could be hidden behind it. I tipped it over, and several of the drawers slid out loudly.

"What's going on in there?" Angel hissed.

"*I'm* okay, in case you were wondering," I said with some irritation, "and it smells awful in here. I should have sent *you* in." There were too many smells to separate and they were all bad so I just called them 'forgotten places' and put that at the bottom of the list.

The goal of all this was taped behind one of the bottom drawers, and I pulled it free. Angel helped me lift the door enough to get out, and I held up the quart jar of dimes like it was the Stanley Cup.

"Change!" she shouted and caught herself.

"All this for *loose change!*" she whispered.

"Not just loose change," I said smugly. "These are old dimes - real silver!"

"Really?" she said. "How much -uh- how much are we talking there?"

I reattached the lock, and we headed for the first camera.

"A dime has a radius of zero point three five two five inches and a thickness of zero point zero five three inches. The volume of a cylinder is the radius squared times pi times the thickness, which means one dime takes up approximately zero point zero two zero seven cubic inches of space. This is a one-quart jar which is fifty-seven cubic inches, so except for air gaps, there are two thousand seven hundred eighty-nine dimes - approximately. That's only two hundred seventy-eight dollars' face value but these are all old, so they're real silver. Each has zero point zero eight troy ounces of silver which is currently trading at about ten dollars an ounce. It's a shame we can't go back a year when it was *thirty-five* dollars an ounce. Oh well, easy money!" I said and held the jar up again - and almost dropped it.

She had a strange expression and finally said, "you really are a robot - from the future."

"What gave it away?" I said sarcastically, "and you forgot *super-intelligent*."

"No, I mean, I knew that already - but. I don't know it's like I'm seeing it all a little more clearly but it's making *less* sense."

Uh oh, I thought. She was probably high most of the time we'd been together at that point. Now her head was clearing, and that could be trouble for me. I might even have to confess to the detox shot I gave her.

After all the cameras had been uncovered, we headed for the center of town. All this exercise was good for her recovery, but I was going to need a serious recharge before long. I had scanned the entire contents of a phone book the night before, so I knew there was an all-night pawn shop, over by the courthouse. We exchanged the dimes for half what they were worth. *Those* guys were the *real* thieves. I wanted to wait until morning and get a better deal at a coin shop, but Angel insisted as soon as she heard the guy say the word *thousand*. She was *not* a good negotiator.

"Okay," I said, "but I hold the money."

That got a snicker from pawn-shop-guy. Angel shot daggers at him, and he almost choked. She was a joy to be around sometimes, but she could also scare the shit out of people. It was like they sensed an *I got nothin' to live for* attitude from just a look. Maybe it was body language. I tried it a few times, but I couldn't pull it off.

~

CHAPTER SUMMARY

Just in case you got called away on a secret mission for six months and couldn't take this book because it would blow your cover as a vulgar tourist, here's where we are:

The untimely death of the Ford Pinto has necessitated the purchase of a new vehicle. Martin has stolen a dead woman's loose change, and Angel has frightened an innocent pawnbroker.

PARADOX BY THE DASHBOARD LIGHT

The junkyard was, of course, on the opposite side of town, so it took another few hours to get there on foot. Even so, it was still dark when we arrived, and we had to wait for the place to open. I outlined my plan to find a car that was about to be crushed and save it. That way, it would have a low domino-count. It would have no future without us intervening, so very little would change as long as we didn't crash it into anything. I wondered if that would work in our favor and whatever mysterious force was at play here would make it uncrashable. A guy in a sleeveless flannel shirt eventually came to unlock the gate - fifteen minutes late. We asked about cars on their last legs, and he showed us a rusty red Fiat that was way too small, a wrecked Chevy Vega, and a ten-year-old Dodge Colt. Angel turned her nose up at all of these. I don't know why I went along with it, but she had assumed the role of car-judge with full veto rights.

"I want *that* one," she said pointing at a 1968 Lincoln Continental with a cracked windshield, no wheels, and several dents. It was black, of course. I don't think they made them in any other color. It had a red leather interior and the iconic 'suicide doors' - rear doors that opened the wrong way out.

"Oh, that's not for the crusher," junkyard-guy explained. "The engine's blown, but it's a classic. I'm going to restore it someday."

I did a quick search through my files and found that it still existed in 2216 in the same location in pretty much the same condition. I guess *someday* never came for this guy. I estimated it to have a low-domino count, so I made Angel wait out of earshot while I haggled. From the way she was pawing at it, she would have just given him all our money for this thing, and it was going to need a lot of parts. While we negotiated, he kept looking over my shoulder at Angel, but every time I turned around, she had a *what-who-me* expression. In the end, he surprised me and settled for half the money we had and *special consideration* on any parts I needed to scrounge from the storeroom or the other cars.

"I'm starving," she shouted at us as we were finishing.

Sleeveless-flannel offered to take her to Denny's, and they left in his pickup truck. They were gone for three hours. By the time they got back, I had a new engine installed and running. I scrounged four matching rims - no easy task - and a set of reasonable tires. I couldn't find a windshield, so I used a laser to melt the glass back together along the crack. It wasn't a perfect fix, but it would do. In the end, it actually took longer to clean the damn thing than to get it running. Goddamn OCD.

"Nice!" she said and walked around it nodding.

"It doesn't smell like possum nest as much - and I added some upgrades too," I said and started the engine remotely.

She gasped and giggled, "what else? Does it fly too?"

"No - it doesn't *fly*. I'm all out of *magic* dust. That's all it does remotely. I didn't have time to make it self-driving yet."

Having experienced her skill at the wheel, that was actually at the top of my list.

"Where's your fiancé?" I said.

"He's taking a nap in the office," she said and leaned in through the open passenger side window to examine the interior.

"Remind me to look into a career as a junkyard guy," I said. "It seems pretty cushy."

"You should have put in a CD player," she was pointing at the hole in the dash.

"Oh, I think we can do better than that," I said and began blasting music to the speakers. It was probably Bruce Springsteen. I hadn't widened her horizons yet, and she was really into him back then.

When it finished, she stopped dancing and shouted, "Where did that come from? Play some more! Play some more!"

"I have every song ever made," I said like it was nothing. I just wanted to see her reaction to having the world's largest record collection. She didn't disappoint. My God, I loved it when she was happy like that. I played something else, and she shoved me hard, so I skipped to the next song which she also didn't like so she pushed me a little more gently. Eventually, she got tired of pushing me and just started yelling, "next!" I zeroed in on her preferences and came up with a stream of oldies from the 80's and also some newer stuff which I thought she'd like.

She got in on the driver's side and shouted at me, "let's go! Let's go! It looks good *enough*!"

I was still pounding out a dent, but she was being impatient, so I got in, and she threw gravel getting it aimed at the exit.

"You might want to go easy on the gas," I shouted. "I put twin superchargers in it, so it's got over seven hundred horsepower."

"Is that a lot?" she shouted back as we hit the street. Her answer came as she slammed her foot to the floor and left two parallel black streaks on the pavement - and then the engine died.

I stopped playing the music and started swearing as it slowly rolled to a stop.

"Well, that was the fastest thirty feet in street racing history," she said and laughed.

I tried to glare at her.

"I don't understand it," I said as I got out and went around to the front. "The engine was solid. If anything, I expected to have trouble with the transmission. That's a lot of extra power."

"It's *so hard* to find a good mechanic these days," she said leaning out the driver's side window.

"Yeah yeah," I said as she pulled the hood release.

It was the throttle linkage. *Just like the Pinto.*

She stuck her head out the window to taunt me some more, "hey it's not self-driving, but it *is* self-stopping!"

I was about to reattach the linkage securely, but then I remembered what happened last time. Instead, I made the flimsiest connection I could and gingerly set the hood down. It latched with a click, and I went around to get back in.

"Is it fixed?" she said.

"Be *very* gentle," I warned, "and turn around. We need to go the other direction."

Angel didn't know the meaning of *gentle*. She turned the wheel hard to the left and floored it again until we did a half-donut and ended up more-or-less pointed in the opposite direction. I refused to play any music until she agreed to settle down and drive at least *close* to the speed limit. This idea of a fuse was fascinating. I wasn't ready to call it fate yet, but it sure seemed like some directions were safer than others. We were passing a hardware store, so I had her pull in.

"I have an idea," I said. "We can't keep patching up whatever kills the engine. If I add a really *weak* part then hopefully, that will be the first thing to fail If it's also easy to reset, we may have a solution."

I went inside and bought a large round button-switch, an electrical breaker, and some wire. My story about being a movie prop didn't go over as well in there, and I got a lot of stares. I guess those guys were a little farther from the gullible end of the spectrum. The third one to ask me, "what are you supposed to be?" got a new answer, "I'm a secret government experiment." They were satisfied with that. So much for skepticism. They just believed a different *flavor* of nonsense. At least nobody called the police.

We stopped at a park so I could install our new breaker. After ten minutes, we had a much *stronger* throttle linkage, a much *weaker* ignition system, and a new red button on the dash where the radio should have been. I connected the breaker to the engine's ignition and ran the reset back to the button on the dash. If the breaker tripped, the engine would stop firing until we pressed the button. It was like trying to run two hair dryers from the same outlet. But instead of having to run all the way down into the basement we just had to press the button on the dash and turn the Lincoln in a different direction. It was on a hair trigger, and I thought it might just trip at random, but it turned out to be pretty stable.

"We should try a few different directions and see what happens," I said, and she started the engine.

"Let's go east," I said in a loud voice.

I don't know If I thought the universe was listening, and I needed to be clear or what, but she put it in gear, and the breaker made a loud pop, and immediately killed the engine.

"Okay," I said. I was actually a little surprised this was working. I also had mixed feelings about it because although it made us a lot safer, it also meant we didn't really have any freewill.

"West?" she suggested.

"Yes, I fully intend to go *west*," I said again loudly and hit the button. She started it again, and we were off. As soon as we reached the edge of town, we tried north and south with no success. Whatever we were supposed to do, or *allowed* to do, it was west, so we kept going.

∾

CHAPTER SUMMARY

Here's where we are so far:

Martin and Angel have now been to both of the bad sides of Dubuque Iowa. A man with no sleeves has sold Martin a classic Lincoln Continental and purchased a Grand Slam breakfast. Martin has restored the Lincoln and modified it to stall at intersections - more than they usually do. Angel has discovered that Martin is a spider-shaped infinite jukebox.

NON-HAUNTED HOUSE

"Hey, I just thought of something," Angel said as we left town. "Nanna's house is east of here. I can't get to her." She sounded really concerned.

"I'm sure she's fine," I said, "and anyway, this won't be forever. Maybe there's something simple we need to do, and then we can go back and check on her. We just need to figure out what's west of here and what it is we're supposed to do."

"Any ideas about that?" she asked

"As a matter of fact, I've been to a place near here before. Hope you like farms."

That damn Temporal Fuse almost killed us twice when it stalled the car at intersections where it wanted us to turn. I know it didn't really have *intention*. It was just a breaker with a high probability of tripping, but it was hard not to ascribe agency to it when it kept making us change direction like that. The other drivers were less than happy with us as we tested each new heading, stalling each time. We eventually made it to a small town ironically called Iowa Falls. As far as I could tell, there was no waterfall. Maybe there was a girl named Iowa, and she fell a lot. As we poked around, we found we could go anywhere inside city limits but trying to leave in any direction tripped the breaker. This confused the hell out of me since the Murphy farm I had been to - wait, would go to - in 1985 was north of Iowa Falls.

"What do you think it means," Angel asked over her breakfast. It was actually noon, but she was still eating like a horse and only wanted breakfast food.

"The farm is pretty close," I said, "so it's obviously why we're here. I think we're too early for what we have to do. We probably have to wait until Thomas comes and leaves. Or maybe we're supposed to hitch a ride with him. I don't know what we do in the meantime, that's three years away, and I'm pretty sure there's no skeeball in this entire town."

"Hey we can buy a lottery ticket and get some money!" she said.

"No," I said trying to be patient, "remember the Pinto, and besides, we can't leave. What are you going to spend it on *here?*"

She frowned and returned to her pancakes.

"Bingo," I said as I found the perfect place for us. I had been searching the RSD data for spare cash and also a place to stay. Iowa Falls didn't have any hotels so renting was the only option. At the edge of town, there was a piece of property nobody wanted. The RSD data showed it was still vacant in 2216. It caught fire during construction, so all that was left was the brick shell and the roof. The newspaper article said, 'Local Boy Returns to Retire.' Apparently, a resident named Dietrich Vogel left to seek his fortune in the Chicago sausage business, and he did pretty well. When he decided to retire, he came back to his hometown and began building a mansion on a hill. It caught fire during construction, and the fire department managed to get the fire out before it damaged the roof, but not before it gutted the first floor and most of the second. The old man died shortly after that. All of this happened in the early seventies. It was a great property with a view of the whole town so, initially, I was surprised that nobody tore it down to build something else. My understanding of psychology at the time was pretty weak. Some more research showed that the entire community thought the place was *cursed* - and since the guy died right afterward - also *haunted*.

"You've got something? Is it treasure? Please let it be treasure!" Angel said.

"Not treasure. You're not afraid of ghosts, or cursed places, are you? On a scale of one to ten, what's your comfort level with sleeping in a place that's definitely not cursed or haunted but other people, less sophisticated than yourself, might *think* was - you known - a little *spooky?*"

"*You* can sleep in the haunted house. *I'll* sleep in the car," she said almost spitting eggs at me.

"Look, this Movie Prop story only works if people see me once or twice. If we're hanging around town all the time, these villagers are going to start gathering torches and pitchforks. We need a place to hide and our options are pretty limited."

A young couple passed our booth on their way out, and the guy was staring at Angel.

"*Your* options are limited," she said to me and winked at him without his girlfriend catching it. "*Mine* aren't."

The waitress came to refill Angel's coffee and eyed me curiously.

"Hey," I said to her, "do you know anything about that property that burned a while back? The owner's name was Vogel."

She crossed herself and made some other intricate gestures before answering, "I know it. Are you making a movie up there?"

That confused me until I remembered that I was a movie prop.

"Please tell my friend here that it's not haunted," I said.

"Oh, it's *definitely* haunted," she said as if it was the most obvious thing in the world. "No one's ever spent the entire night there - and lived. At least, that's what they say."

"That's not true," I said. "Nobody has ever died or disappeared there. That's all campfire stories."

"Old Dietrich died up there," she said. "Something scared him to death right before, whatever it was, burned the place to the ground. He refused to tell anybody what he saw that night."

"Wait, how was he supposed to say *anything* if he was already dead

- and if he died in the house how did he get out before it burned - and the paper said he died in a hospital in Dubuque a week later. None of this makes any sense."

"Don't believe everything you read," she said. "His bones are still up there somewhere," she tore our check off a pad and slapped it on the table.

My mind was still trying to unravel that tangled story when Angel surprised me and suggested that we go and have a look for ourselves.

"If you're afraid it's haunted," I said, "which I shouldn't have to point out, is *not a real thing - ever* - wouldn't you want to stay as far away as possible?"

She ignored me, scooted to the edge of the bench and stood up, "you're buying, right?"

"I didn't even eat anything!" I said.

"Come on, let's go. We'll be fine. It's daylight. The spirits have no power during the day - but I'm not going *inside*."

～

We caught our first glimpse of it as we rounded the last corner. The place was a wreck. It was at the top of a steep hill and the driveway curved down to a locked gate at the street. That was the only gap in a six-foot high, brick wall that encompassed the five-acre property. We stood there for a while and took it all in. The massive yard was all weeds and trash but no trees. Each of the window-shaped openings on the ground floor had a crown of black soot above it - but no glass. The windows probably hadn't been installed yet when the place burned. The second-floor windows looked a little better, and the roof looked fine. Off to the side was a three-car garage with a stairway on the side - probably a maid's suite.

"Yep, that's definitely haunted," she said and motioned to the gate. "Pick the lock. I want to get a closer look."

"That's just stupid," I said as I worked on the rusty lock. "First of all - ghosts aren't real, and if they were, you wouldn't be able to tell from *here*."

"It's a feeling you get," she said smugly. "I'm very sensitive to these things."

The lock was being stubborn. Just once, I'd like to find one that's not all rusty and have somebody say, *if only a hero would come along and get that clean and well-lubricated lock open, we'd all be saved!* I finally got it open, and we headed up the curved driveway. I kept looking behind us thinking somebody might care that we were trespassing. Angel kept her eyes locked on the creepy house. She stopped a few feet from the front porch steps.

"How about this: we can rent the maid's apartment above the garage," I said. "It can't possibly be haunted. I can use the main house as a workshop. The basement is probably in good shape."

~

CHAPTER SUMMARY

Here's where we are so far:

Angel has realized that they are unable to return to her grand-mother's house. Martin has revealed that he has been to rural Iowa before - in the future. They have arrived at Iowa Falls, a town named after a clumsy girl, and found that they cannot leave the town without tripping the Temporal Fuse. With no hotels in town, they have been forced to seek an alternative that is definitely not haunted.

UNLUCKY RABBIT'S EAR

After a little asking around, we landed at *Templeton Realty/Insurance/Property Management and Estate Planning.* For such a long name, it sure was a small place. We were greeted by a balding, pudgy man in a light gray suit. Apparently, he did all the *lawyery* stuff for everyone in town and dabbled in Real Estate as well. He took us into a side office so we could *talk privately.* I looked around the empty waiting room wondering who he expected to interrupt us. I stood, and Angel sat at one of the chairs across the desk from him, as he got comfortable.

"Now, what can I do for you?" he asked.

He tactfully hadn't asked about me yet, so I volunteered it, "as you can see I'm a movie prop," I said, and he nodded seriously, "and we're scouting locations to shoot a few scenes for our next project. We're looking at a lot of different places and thought we'd inquire about the Vogel house. I understand you manage it for the heirs?"

"I do."

"Wonderful," I said. "We'd be looking at a three-year lease with an option to extend."

He held out his palms facing us and said, "I'm afraid we're only entertaining offers for purchase at this time."

I have great self-control, or I would have laughed. Angel seemed amused by this too, but she only smiled.

"We're only making a *movie*," I said. "We don't need to *buy* it."

"I'm sorry, but I don't think that's going to be possible," he said.

I was about to corral him with some logic about the realities of trying to sell a property in that condition - in rural Iowa, when Angel stood and rounded the desk. She took his tie in her hand and gently pulled his face close to hers. I thought she was going to kiss him, but instead, she moved to his ear and whispered something salacious. This poor guy looked like a snared rabbit. She released him and sat on the edge of the desk to wait for his answer.

"Wuh - uh - I'm - I think we can," he cleared his throat and started again, "I think the owners might be amenable to taking on some short-term caretakers - in order to improve the property for eventual sale," he was talking himself into it. "You'd have to stay in the maid's apartment above the garage. It's - the only living space approved by the county for habitation. I'm legally obligated to warn you to stay out of the main house for your own safety," he said and winked at me.

"Short term?" I said. "We might need it long-term - you know for sequels and whatnot."

He looked at Angel, and she leaned in to whisper something else, but he backed away and held up a hand. "I'm sure we can work something out. I'll offer the idea to the heirs of the estate with some wording about 'until a viable offer has been made.' We all know that's never going to happen, so that would make it *effectively* long-term."

"Perfect," I said, and Angel bounced off the desk clapping her hands with excitement.

He gave us keys and Angel signed a contract which stated vaguely that we would *improve the property* in return for lodging.

We returned to the mansion, and I rummaged around in the basement for raw materials while Angel cleaned the one-bedroom efficiency apartment above the detached garage. When I went to check on her, she was sitting on the couch watching TV, working her way through a Tootsie Pop. As far as I could tell, nothing was any cleaner, but at least the washer was running so she must have started on the towels and sheets. The apartment had that now-familiar forgotten places smell but not as bad as the main house. I found the vacuum, but it was dirty, so I cleaned it. Then I used *it* to clean everything *else* - and then cleaned the vacuum again while she watched me with curiosity.

"I'm hungry," she said pausing her progress on another sucker, "and there's no food."

"Well, I have a lot more to do. Why don't you go into town and get groceries?"

She held out her hand, and when I didn't respond, she snapped her fingers and made repetitive curling motions with her fingers.

"I'll need some *money*," she said finally.

"What happened to the money I gave you?"

"What money? Come on, Martin. I'm hungry."

Something about hearing her use my name hijacked my brain, and I pushed aside the polka dot dress to get at the pocket in my overalls. I pulled out the last of my money.

"I need some clothes too," she said and snatched the entire roll before I had a chance to split it up.

"Go easy on the Lincoln!" I shouted as she bounced down the steps outside the apartment. "And be careful - remember the dominos!"

I don't know exactly what I meant by that. Apparently, we were supposed to do - or not do - something, but without knowing what, it would be hard to be *careful* about it.

While she was gone, I washed the dishes - and the cabinets. This place was covered in a layer of dust that seemed to be everywhere. I finished washing the towels and linens before turning my attention to something more productive. Angel was going to be a problem if I kept letting her go to town alone, so as much as I hated the idea of doing anything on Thomas's list, I was going to have to make an effort to *blend in*. The construction crew had left a treasure trove of half-burned tools and supplies in the basement of the main house. My first priority was a bit of body shaping. Clothes would cover most of me, so a human*oid* shape was all I needed for now - and maybe a hat and sunglasses. Under the ladybug dress, I was still wearing the railroad engineer's costume Thomas had made for me. It was blue and white striped overalls with so many pockets that I was still finding new ones. I loved all the pockets, so I wasn't about to let go of them yet. The two legs farthest back had actual full-length tubes of fabric, but the other six just had openings. I figured I could safety pin those closed and look more or less normal.

Angel returned with groceries and a bad mood. She had tried to find some clothes that were up to her standards, but it was a small town, and there was only one little shop that sold clothes. She was forced to buy conservative things - and a pair of scissors.

I forced myself to sit and watch TV with her after dinner. It was painful. Entertainment in this time period was about as good as gourmet food a thousand years ago - predictable and bland. She finally went to bed, and I started my projects.

There was a one-hundred-foot tunnel connecting a trap-door in the floor of the garage to the basement of the main house. Angel didn't know about it, and I wasn't ready to tell her yet. She would've freaked out if she knew the two buildings were connected in any way, infecting *her* apartment with the *hauntedness* of the house. Maybe ghosts needed tunnels for some reason? I was fuzzy on the whole ghost-physics thing.

Body shaping went pretty fast since I just needed to fold away a few limbs and pound my roundish form into more of a human-shaped torso. Also, my arms and legs were connected to my thorax section leaving a big fat abdomen just hanging off the end there. That was anatomically correct for a spider but not very practical. Thomas never let practicality get in the way of authenticity. I merged the thorax and abdomen before moving all my legs around. In the end, I thought I had something pretty convincing until I looked in a mirror. My head was still very spidery. I had two quarter-sized black eyes, more-or-less in the right spot, but they were flanked on each side by a pair of smaller dime-sized eyes. I take back what I said about Thomas's authenticity and practicality. There's one thing that trumped both of those for him - whimsy. He had added two bushy eyebrows, locked in a pathetic *surprised* position. I had no actual mouth, but a black line gave the illusion of a permanent frown.

~

The next morning, I presented myself to her for inspection. "What do you think?"

She giggled, "well it's not bad. If you put some clothes on, it'll do from a distance, but I don't know about your head."

I had beaten it into a more human, and less basketball, shape but it was still metal.

"It's a work in progress," I said.

She glanced down, "not anatomically correct either."

"I'm not going out *naked*. I think I'll manage."

She shrugged, "so what's next. When can we leave?" She was getting bored with that town already and we'd only been there a day.

"I got the mower running," I said.

"So?"

"So we have to look like caretakers," I said. "It's a rider. All you have to do is sit and steer." I really just wanted to tidy up the yard. Goddamn OCD.

"Me!" she said genuinely shocked that I would even suggest it. "I don't know how to mow a lawn," she said and crossed her arms.

"I think you can figure it out."

To sweeten the pot, I gave her the world's first Bluetooth earbuds. I'm pretty sure I didn't violate the patent since they weren't going to be invented for another fifteen years.

"While you're doing that, I'll come up with a way for you to check on Granny."

"Nanna?" she shouted, her mood suddenly brighter.

"But it's going to take a while. I have to build a few things, so you mow, I'll build. Deal?"

I held out a ball cap to her.

She sighed and took it. As I worked, I checked on her every few minutes. She was even smiling some of the time. Maybe the mindless tedium was hypnotizing her. She got about half done and began screaming my name. I dropped my tools and ran from the garage toward the shrieking. She met me in the middle of the freshly cut section. Her shirt was off, and she was holding it in front of her. It was covered in blood. I thought she'd cut herself or something.

"What is it? Are you hurt?" I shouted already flipping through possible scenarios and how to fix them with my meager medical ability. I was pretty sure I couldn't re-attach a hand.

She was unintelligible, "I didn't mean to," she said between sobs, "it just jumped in the way!" she took a breath in shudders. "I couldn't stop. You have to fix it, Martin!"

I examined her hands, and they were fine, so I gently pried them open to look inside the bloody shirt she was holding. There was a lot of fur and gore. It was a rabbit, dead beyond all repair. But something underneath was still moving. I took the shirt away from her and set it on the ground to have a closer look. Underneath its dead mother, was a baby missing one ear but otherwise whole and alive.

"Okay," I said, "I'm sorry, I can't do anything for the mother, but I can sew up the baby's head, and he'll be fine with one ear."

"No," she said firmly and took another staccato gasp, "no - you have to fix him. It's my fault. You have to fix him!"

"Angel," I said slowly, "it's not your fault." I wanted to add, *and it's just a rabbit - people eat them*, but I didn't dare say it.

"You're right!" she said. "It's *your* fault. *You* made me mow the Goddamn grass!"

That didn't take long, I thought, but then she surprised me.

"Oh Martin, I'm sorry! Please fix him. Please. I'll do anything you want."

I sighed, "okay - no promises, but I'll see what I can do about the ear. You go shower and try to calm down."

I gave the bunny a shot to keep it from going into shock and went to examine the scene of the crime. It was pretty bad. Murdered rabbits are not a good smell. I made a mental note to avoid sharing that with Angel. I picked through the remnants and came up with an ear that was *probably* his. The mower got his mother and one of his siblings. I looked up 'rabbit litter size' in my files - *holy crap* 'one to fourteen with an average of six.' Sure enough, I found three more in the tall grass. I took them all back to the garage and sewed the ear back on with cotton thread - not the best thing to use, but good enough if I could keep it from getting infected. A cardboard box was preventing the others from wandering off, and I added their unconscious brother as Angel came around from the apartment stairs. She was wearing the clothes she bought the day before. They hadn't been chopped up yet, so she actually looked like a normal person. It was strange to see her like that in jeans and a tee-shirt. She was still crying, so I was going to have to get some fluids into her before dehydration set in.

"Is he fixed?"

"Good as new," I said. "Well, the ear might flop around, but it's attached. He'll be fine."

She hugged me and wiped her eyes. I sat her down and brought the box of bunnies to her. She started crying again and picking each one up to apologize for - and I quote "murdering your mother" - yeah, that's exactly what she said. We went up to the apartment, and I made her drink two full glasses of water, pulling one bunny after another out of her hands so she could drink.

"We need four baby bottles," she said, "and diapers. And a playpen. And car seats."

"That's ridiculous," I said. "First of all, they're probably weaned already, and there's no way I'm making tiny car seats for rabbits."

"Fine, I'll do it myself," she said and stood up. "I'm going to the store," she took the box of bunnies and tromped down the stairs to the car.

"I thought you didn't have any money!" I shouted, but she ignored me.

I did my best to hose down the bloody spot in the yard and finished mowing. There *was* something hypnotic about doing something tedious and repetitive. After that, I returned my attention to my new project: a 3-D printer. Ultimately, I wanted to make a quad-copter capable of going beyond the edge of town. There wasn't much of the construction equipment I could use unmodified, but with the addition of some of my parts from one leg, I was able to come up with a workable device. That leg would just need some replacements once the printer was operational.

Angel returned two hours later with a playpen, bottles, cloth diapers, and several bags of various things. I wondered what the good townsfolk thought of her wandering up and down the grocery store with a box of rabbits. The diapers were too big, so she cut them down and managed to get one on each of the bunnies. They looked ridiculous, and I know a little bit about whimsical costumes. I studied under the master. After she made me sit and watch while she paraded all the things she bought, it was my turn. I went down to the garage where my 3-D printer was just finishing up the last of four bunny-sized car seats. I know it was stupid, but it wasn't actually that much work. I just took a basic design, scaled it down, and the printer did the rest. She was over the moon. The seats could also be connected side-by-side for fastening to the backseat of the Lincoln using the seat belts.

"They'll probably fit in the shopping cart too!" she said.

"I'll take your word for that. I don't think I want to see that level of crazy."

That evening we watched TV again, this time with the bunnies in Angel's lap. Afterward, she insisted on them sleeping in her bed, which made me cringe.

It took me all night and all the next day, but I got my first-edition drone finished. It was just a standard early-twenty-first-century quadcopter, but I added two RSD mods. Reggie's Remote-Sensor-Device, or RSD, was one of his first inventions and it was simple enough that I could recreate it from the designs. He used it to gather the Earth survey data that we had been using to find lost treasures and dirty five-dollar bills. I was proud of the fact that I came up with a new use for the technology. I found that if I went deeper and probed the liquid metal outer core of the Earth, the data I got back was uninteresting, but I also got a strong, changing magnetic field. All I had to do was add a coil and hey-presto! Free electricity! I managed to produce a passable seven-inch LCD screen. Those things were hard to make! And even as small as it was, it had several dead pixels that I just couldn't get right. I also added a claw for petty thievery. There was a lot of junk in the basement, but there were still things I was going to have to scrounge from town.

∾

CHAPTER SUMMARY

Here's where we are so far:

Martin has proposed leasing the local haunted house, and the initially reluctant realtor has been moved by Angel's detailed description of all the things that she could do to the property, despite its age. Angel and Martin have taken on the roles as caretakers in exchange for lodging above the detached, and definitely not haunted, garage. Martin has violated a copyright and Angel has committed a double murder. Martin has sharpened his home-surgery skills. Angel has adopted orphaned rabbits, and Martin has created a drone.

PIZZA WITH EXTRA SAUSAGE

"Show me what you got," Angel said.

We were at the kitchen table of the apartment watching the tiny display. I was giving general instructions to the drone, but it was on its own as far as obstacle avoidance. The display showed countryside sweeping past fifty feet below as it flew eastward.

"It's a drone. Cross your fingers that it doesn't encounter a mysterious and unlikely failure. It should be at *Banana's* house in another five minutes," I said.

"Nanna," she corrected and began bringing the bunnies over and changing their diapers one by one, fitting each of them into his car seat - *on the kitchen table.* Disgusting. I was going to have to buy more bleach. Angel arranged them in front of the tiny screen to see. They ignored it of course and munched away at their lettuce. They *were* weaned, as I suspected, but that didn't keep Angel from trying to give them milk from tiny bottles. Who knows where she found those. They were probably for dolls. The drone reached the edge of town, and I pulled the screen away from the disinterested rodents.

"I gave it Granny's address so it should just hover in the street when it gets there," I said.

The drone came to a stop amid the sea of rooftops and descended over the center of the road. At about twenty feet above the ground, we could see a front porch. It was pointed at the neighbor across the street from our target, so I sent it a command to turn. After a short lag, it revealed Nanna's house and Angel gasped. It had only been two days. I wondered why she was so excited. I guess the fact that she couldn't visit in person made it special. There was an old car in the driveway. It had a colorful sign on the roof that advertised, "Tony's Pizza!"

"Well she's not eating *better,* but at least it's something besides corn chips," I said.

As the drone got closer to the porch, we saw that the front door was open, but the screen door obscured the view of the living room. The quadcopter had active-noise-cancellation, but it wasn't perfect. I thought she might come out to see what the humming sound was. She didn't. I had it slide to the side window for a better view and instantly regretted it. Her hair was still gray but only at the ends. The rest was growing in blonde, and the wrinkles were gone. She looked twenty - at least, the parts I could see. The naked pizza guy was blocking my view - yeah. Angel shielded the eyes of the bunny's and spun them around which I thought was pretty funny. Her mouth was wide open, but she said nothing for a several seconds.

"Stop, stop, stop. Turn it away," she waved her hands at the screen.

I pulled the drone back to the street, unsure what to do next. Angel turned to me with a mixture of anger and shock.

"What - was that?" she demanded.

"Oh, yeah that's probably my fault," I said. "Hey, I was in a hurry! I searched for 'Iron and vitamins,' and the first thing that came up was something called a *standard health cocktail,* so that's what I gave her. I read the details just now, and it says it also *mends any age-related damage.* Oops."

"You made my Nanna immortal!"

"No - not immortal, she's just - young again. It's like a reset button."

And that's when it hit me. That was a lot of dominos, and she looked *just* like Angel. I mean they could have been twins and from what I saw with pizza-guy, behavior too. *She* was the overdose victim in my files. The cops must have known Angel and just misidentified. If they took fingerprints, they would have just assumed it was an error in the files. I did my best to hide my shock at this. I'm also ashamed to say I was a little relieved. It meant Angel was safe.

"Well, she's healthy and happy - *very* happy by the looks of it. I say we give her some privacy and get on with our mission."

"Ew!" she said and repeated it a few more times, "Ew. Ew. Ew!"

"Um, I should probably check you too."

"Why? What did you do to *me*?" she said and narrowed her eyes.

They say confession is good for the soul, but I can tell you, it's pretty hard on the body sometimes. She pushed me so hard I would have broken a few bones if I wasn't made of metal. I told her everything - her addiction problem and the injection I gave her, my neutralizing her entire stash, and the worst of it -the part about the coroner's report and my theory about Nanna's impending doom. If I was right, there was nothing we could do about it, but she didn't hear that or didn't care. She shouted something about not being the one with a problem, scooped up the rack of bunnies and stormed out. I thought she was just going for a walk in the night air to cool off until I heard the Lincoln's engine roar to life. I ran after her, but she had too much of a head start on me. The drone was still too far away to be of any help. It didn't matter. I knew she was trying to get back to Nanna's. As I approached the edge of town, I saw the car stalled in the middle of the road with the hood up. Angel was leaning in and doing something to the engine. Before I could reach her, she slammed the hood down, jumped back in, and was off again. She hot-wired my fuse. Angel could be very clever when she wanted to. I think the superchargers might have been a mistake because running after her was causing my power cell to heat up. I knew I wouldn't be able to run all the way to Dubuque, but I didn't have to. She crashed into a tree on the other side of a tight curve. As I got closer, I saw one of the wheels had come completely off. I caught up with her as she was limping down the road clutching those ridiculous rabbits. I guess they actually *did* need car seats. I took them from her. She collapsed to the ground and began sobbing. I searched my files for the appropriate thing to say - a magical incantation that would make her happy again, but there was nothing. I took one of the bunnies out of its car seat and handed it to her. She pressed it to her face so hard I thought she might crush it.

"Come on. It's past their bedtime. Let's go home."

She was exhausted and banged up, so I carried her. That took quite a while since I had to take the *scenic route* - through the woods. I was afraid if we stayed on the road, some Samaritan would stop and try to help us. Now humans in this time had no problem with other people who look *exactly* human. They also had no problem with furniture and other things that were *obviously* not human. In-between, however, is something they called the "uncanny valley" where things that look *sort-of* human are met with screams, running, and gunfire. I was *mayor* of Uncanny Valley.

It was almost dawn by the time we got home. I put Angel and her brood to bed and recharged myself before setting about cleaning the mud off my *everything*.

～

CHAPTER SUMMARY

Here's where we are so far:

Martin's drone has made its debut and needs a thorough lens-cleaning. Nanna still isn't getting out much, but she has improved her diet - slightly. Martin has confessed to Angel about accidentally curing Nanna of everything and curing Angel of the problem she definitely doesn't have. Angel has shown that she can hot-wire a Temporal Fuse, the bunnies have crash-tested the car seats, and the Lincoln is as dead as Abraham.

TWENTY-FOUR HORSES TOO MANY

The Lincoln was totaled, so I didn't bother trying to get it back. The cops probably towed it to its most recent owner of record - sleeveless flannel - and he probably parked it in the same exact spot waiting for *someday*. Instead, I rummaged around at the local junkyard and found a rusty and dented, engineless Volkswagen bus that looked promising. I was all out of money and Iowa Falls was too small to have any fast-food or drive-through banking, so another "fence run" wasn't possible. I needed an alternative, so I combed through the RSD data again. The very same junkyard held the solution to my problem. It was in an old sailboat, way in the back. I wondered where you could use a sailboat in Iowa. I guess Lake Michigan isn't that far away. Anyway, this thing had a keel with ballast made of lead under the galley floor, and somebody had carved away enough of the soft metal to stash a small lockbox. I paid a midnight visit and found it with no trouble at all. There was a bundle of around fifty-thousand dollars in there, but I only took two thousand to pay for the van and some parts. I still didn't trust Angel with large amounts of cash, although this did seem to be a turning point for her. After the crash - or maybe it was the rabbits - anyway, she seemed to be calming down. She even started dressing in normal clothes more and more.

While I was at the junkyard, I found an engine in decent condition. It was in a crashed Beetle. They actually used the same engine in those days - can you believe it? It only had twenty-five horsepower - *twenty-five*! I was going to miss the Lincoln. All of the things I could think of to get more horsepower into it would have created a heat problem, so I had to leave it alone. Angel didn't care about speed. Like I said, she was changing. I think in her mind she envisioned taking the rabbits everywhere she went, and she felt a little ashamed of almost killing them in the Lincoln. According to her, "one horse, all by itself, could probably tow the van, so it actually had twenty-four more than it needed." Ridiculous. I fitted it with another Temporal Fuse, and after it was fixed up, we took it out for a test drive. It did the same thing the Lincoln did when we tried to leave town. We were still stuck there, but I had another idea that would make it tolerable for both of us.

"Hey, have I ever told you how nice the future is?" I asked.

We were sitting at the table in the tiny kitchen. She just looked at me and kept eating her eggs. It seemed like she had given up. At least she was eating, and she wasn't trying to kill me. I pressed on.

"Well, since you insist, I'll tell you all about it. First of all, nobody has to work at a job they don't enjoy. Now that I think about it, I never heard of anybody having one they *liked* either," she was not impressed by this. I don't think she ever had a real job. In fact, I don't think she ever understood why anybody would subject themselves to employment even in her time. "But that doesn't matter," I said. "They don't need them - because - *money has no value.*"

That got her attention, and she stopped eating for a few seconds. She squinted at me and stuffed a shred of toast in her mouth.

"That's just stupid," she said *with her mouth full*. I think she did that just to annoy me. Talking with her mouth full irritated me, and I may have mentioned it once or twice to her. Probably more than that.

"*I'm crappin' ya negative,*" I said and waited for recognition.

Crickets.

"*Raising Arizona!*" I shouted, but I don't think she got to the movies very often.

"Oh wait," I said after I checked my files. "That doesn't come out for another five years. Sorry. Anyway, in the future, they have these things called Stitchers. It's basically an appliance that makes things for you. Anything you want - food, clothes, vodka, toys, games, houses, flying cars, vodka."

"You said vodka twice," she said.

That made me smile - well *inside* I was smiling. I still couldn't *actually* do it. She was starting to engage, and I think the idea of an achievable paradise was just what she needed.

I shrugged, "they seem to like it. Everybody lives in nice big houses in beautiful places, mostly by the ocean, and they just play games and have parties all day - so lots of vodka."

The problem with pulling someone out of a depression is that they really really want to stay there, and sure enough, she snapped right back in.

"Doesn't matter. I'm stuck here where everything is shitty."

"Not necessarily," I said. "I might be able to get us there. What do you say? You want to go to paradise with me?"

She looked over at the bunnies in their car seats - on - the - table - *again*.

"Forget the rabbits. They need to be released in the woods anyway. How can they reach their full bunny potential riding around with us all the time? They need to run free!" She wasn't buying it, "hop free?" These stupid little rodents were the only good thing in her life, and she wasn't ready to give them up yet.

"Okay, okay," I said, "they can come too."

She raised one eyebrow and pushed her lower lip up as she considered it, "all right, I'll go if they can come too."

I clapped my hands together, but they were metal, so the resulting *clank* wasn't the dramatic effect I had hoped for.

"Excellent! I'll get started right away!"

~

CHAPTER SUMMARY

Here's where we are so far:

Angel has spiraled into a depression. Martin has restored a classic Volkswagen Bus, tempted Angel with an image of a beautiful future, and struggled with OCD in a house full of rodents.

A DOG NAMED SISPOD

I showed Angel the tunnel to the mansion. I think the lack of ghostly visitations eased her mind about the hauntedness of the main house, and I eventually got her to go all the way through the tunnel, but only after I installed blindingly bright lights all the way down its length.

Over the next week, I worked on my project, and she did nothing as far as I could tell. She had picnics with the rabbits every day until a hawk took too much of an interest in them.

"Bring out your queen bee. I need it to steal a shotgun for me."

"It's a *drone*, not a queen bee, and it doesn't steal things," I said.

I had been using it almost exclusively to steal things. Is it stealing if you leave cash behind? Anyway, the idea of Angel with a firearm chilled me, so I lied and said I didn't know how to make one. It wasn't beyond her ability to find something in town, though, so I began checking the van after every trip she made. I must have missed it somehow because she killed that hawk with the first shot. I had cameras and microphones at the corners of the wall that surrounded the five-acre property, so I heard it loud and clear even from the basement and ran up to see Angel standing on a blanket in the grass, prop-ping the butt of a shotgun on her hip. A tiny puff of smoke from the *smokeless* powder was drifting from the barrel.

"What the hell, Angel!" I shouted.

"Nobody messes with my kids," she said and took a bite from the apple in her other hand.

I calmed down a bit and reviewed the feed from the cameras. I let it play in my head a few times. It was a pretty long shot, and she nailed it the first time.

"Well, we're still here, so I guess it wasn't a very important hawk. Nice shot by the way."

"Thanks. First time. I guess I have a natural knack for it."

"Yeah. Natural. Exactly," I said. "If you're done shooting up the place, I have something to show you."

She held the apple in her mouth while she loaded the bunnies back onto the blanket and tied it around her neck.

"*I don't want to sound like a broken horse* here, but you know they're going to need to be set free at some point," I said.

"Just as soon as I kill all the coyotes," she said and winked at me.

"Where did you get that anyway?"

"I know a guy."

~

It was the size and shape of a phone booth. In fact, that's what I started with. It didn't exist in my files from 2216, so it didn't have a high domino count. I stole it from Main Street in the middle of the night. There was a lot of noise involved, but not even one car came by. Either everybody in town slept in a coma, or the universe didn't want them to interfere. I liked the way the door opened, so I kept that part, but I replaced all the glass with sheet metal.

"It's a Stasis-Pod," I said and waited for the adulation from Angel.

She just looked at it and then at me, "what does a - *Stay Sispod* - do?"

"It keeps you in stasis! Just like in Sci-Fi stories," I said searching for a crumb of recognition.

Crickets.

I sighed and gave her the elevator-pitch in monotone, "it wraps you in a null-time field and keeps you from aging while you go into the future. You get in, you come right out, and it's the future."

"It's a time machine!" she said finally excited.

"Uh, Sorta," I said, "it only goes forward, though."

"Who would want to go *back*?" she said.

I think she was serious. It really didn't occur to her why anybody would have any interest in the past. Forward was all that mattered. The past was just a big pile of mistakes and lost opportunities.

"How does it work?" she asked circling it and dragging her fingertips over the smooth surfaces.

"A matrix of lasers superheats the space between the occupant and the outside universe, isolating the inside, forming a small subset-universe..."

"No," she interrupted me, "I mean do you just get in and get out, or is there a button to press or a timer or something? How do you tell it how far to go?"

She was never going to be interested in this stuff. I don't know why I bothered. I sighed again, and she noticed my disappointment.

"...and also how does it manage to do this amazing thing, Martin? I'm interested in that too."

No, she wasn't, but feigned interest was good enough for me.

"It's like you're on an inner tube," I said with renewed enthusiasm, "floating down a river."

"That sounds like fun," she said.

"No-no, it's just a metaphor," I said. "Anyway, the river is *time*, and normally we're just drifting along. Using the Stasis-Pod would be like getting out of the water for a while."

She frowned, "Wouldn't that leave you stuck on the riverbank while everybody else floated by into the future. You'd be stranded in the past."

I had to think about that one. The metaphor seemed solid to me until she said that.

"Okay, maybe it's a bad metaphor..."

"Is the *river* - time," she said, "or is the *bank?* Because we're going past trees, so the ones we've already gone by are *in the past,* and the ones ahead of us are the future, so if we get out..."

I was *sure* this thing would work and had even tested it on clocks - and a banana. The control-banana on the shelf was all brown, but the one inside came out yellow. I *was* sure it worked, but now she was making me nervous.

"I just need a better metaphor," I said. "How about this: there's a force pulling us toward the future, and it's pulling really hard, but our three spatial dimensions are causing drag, so we usually go at a nice slow pace. This machine gets rid of the drag, so we go faster - into the future."

She was still frowning. "Aren't metaphors supposed to use everyday experience to make new things *clearer?*" she said.

"Forget about *how* it works then. Are you ready?"

"Have you tested it yet?" she asked.

"Yeah, but we need a live animal test. I need a guinea pig or similar rodent."

Her eyes narrowed, and I looked around for the shotgun.

"It was a joke!" I said. "Relax! But seriously, how do you feel about grasshoppers?"

"I like them more than *spiders,*" she said still fuming.

"I never was a *real* spider. You know that, right?" I said and retrieved a glass jar from the shelf. The metal lid had several nail-holes poked into it. Inside, was a large green grasshopper.

"Do we have to?" she said peering into the jar.

"Unless *you'd* like to be the first animal test?"

"Nope. Throw him in," she said with a wave of her hand.

I placed the jar on the floor of the booth and closed the door. It made a loud double *clunk-clunk* as it finished sealing. I had made a control panel on the side from a plastic calculator. It had three lights above a numeric keypad. The red light went dark as I entered sixty on the keypad. When I tapped the 'Enter' button, the green light came on, and I stepped back.

"What now?" Angel asked.

"Now we wait. I set it for one minute with a zero-second delay. When we use it ourselves, we'll need to add a delay so we can get inside before it comes on."

"Should I take a good book?" she asked.

"No, I don't think you're getting how this works," I started to say, but when I turned to look at her, she was grinning.

"Stop messing with me. I'm really proud of this," I said.

"I know, Martin. It's amazing. It is," she said.

...but then the timer finished, the yellow light blinked, the door opened - and we saw the jar. It was a mess. The grasshopper had bashed himself against the lid so many times that he was dead. I had used a nail to make the holes in the jar lid, and that always makes the inside surface all jagged and tetanus-ey. Angel picked up the jar and examined it wrinkling her nose.

"Okay," I said, "I think it was just stressed because we ripped it out of its universe. The trip to the future was no problem it was just the beginning - probably."

"*Probably?*" she said. "I'm not getting in that thing."

"*Keep your shirt off*, Angel. I'll fix it," I said.

"On," she corrected.

"What?"

"It's 'keep your shirt *on*,' Martin."

"What did I say?"

Angel laughed, "You said *off.*"

She was right, I did. I wondered what other things I was getting wrong. More of Thomas's pranks no doubt. Bastard.

"Whatever," I said. "Anyway, we just need to sedate any animals, so they don't freak out. I'll find something to use as anesthesia. Can you catch another grasshopper?"

Angel left to find our next victim, and I rummaged around in the garage. I found a can of Starting-Ether. People used it back then to restart their crappy, unreliable motors after they stalled at intersections - which they all seemed to do, all the time - even without a Temporal Fuse to blame. I returned to the basement with my prize and Angel was already waiting with a new grasshopper.

"Wow, you're better at that than *I* was. It took *me* an hour to catch one."

"Some spider you are," she said.

"I'm only using two legs these days, and those damn things are *fast*," I said. "I think I only got that last one because he was tired."

I sprayed a tiny bit of the ether into a new jar and Angel dropped him in. I showed her the lid. "No holes this time."

A repeat of the previous experiment yielded much better results. She insisted on releasing the grasshopper after he woke up. I told her I had some last-minute adjustments to make and we should wait until morning for our trip. Once she was asleep, I tested it on a mouse that I had managed to catch. Catching mice is a lot easier than catching grasshoppers. I was keeping him in the cabinet where Angel wouldn't find him. His trip was an hour long, and he was fine, so I released him in the yard with a big piece of cheese and a great story to tell. Then I tested one of the bunnies - also fine. I was ready for Angel. I gave her a sedative while she was still asleep and placed her in the booth - that was no easy feat. I had to put it on its side and jam the door, so it would stay open while I loaded Angel and the bunnies into it. It looked a little too much like a coffin after I added a cushion and a pillow, so I took them back out. Once Angel was inside and out cold, I ethered-up the bunnies and placed them on her belly before closing the door. I wasn't going along on *this* trip.

The phone booth was still on its side when she awoke, so she banged her head trying to sit up and started swearing at me. I came around from behind it and into her view.

"Who the hell are you?" she demanded.

"Surprise!" I said.

"Martin? What did you do to your head?"

"I upgraded! What do you think? It's Brad Pitt!"

It wasn't until that moment that I realized she had no idea who that was.

Her head was clearing enough to remember *not* getting in the Stasis-Pod voluntarily. "Did you just drug me and throw me in that thing?" she was getting angry.

"Now - Angel - Settle down," I was backing away. "It was all for the best. Everybody came through just fine see?" I pointed at the rabbits.

She glanced over at them. They were munching on something leafy and watching us.

"What year is it? How long were we in there?" she demanded.

"I - didn't actually go in myself - but I will next time. I promise. It's only been a year."

"Martin, so help me, if you ever drug me again…" she heard a scraping sound from behind her and turned around to see what it was.

~

CHAPTER SUMMARY

Here's where we are so far:

A secret tunnel has become less so. Angel has killed a hawk with an illegal firearm. Martin has committed felonious midnight requisition. A phone booth has been made useful. Martin has shown that he's *not* good at metaphors. Angel has shown that she *is* good at catching grasshoppers. Martin has pushed Angel and the rabbits one year into the future and given himself a makeover.

MOSTLY HUMAN

The Stasis-Pod was on its side and resting on the workbench in the center of the room. So, Angel couldn't see the floor behind it. When she peered around and saw the back half of the workshop, she flinched back and reached for the rabbits while keeping her eyes on all the activity going on over there. The floor was a mass of squirming and swarming things of various sizes all crawling over each other. I loved it. The whole thing was a knot of fascinating activity. I could stare at it for hours. Angels reaction was a little different. Her stream of profanity was impressive.

"Relax," I said, "they're mine. It's just a bunch of robots. Watch this!" I held out both hands, palms out, and shouted, "stop!" Everything froze. A few unbalanced things fell over. "Pretty cool huh! I didn't really have to do the hand thing or the shouting. That was just for dramatic effect."

"What is all that?" she demanded.

"I call it Step-Down Near-Nano Tech."

"Well, that just rolls off the tongue," she said sarcastically.

"All I had to do was build a one-quarter-scale pair of hands that I can control remotely and a pair of cameras which I can see through. I used those to cast and shape metal into a set of quarter-scale tools.

Then I use those new tools to make another generation of even smaller hands and eyes, and repeat - easy!"

"And what is the point of *small* robots? Are you going to take over an ant hill?"

I smiled. "Do you like my hair?" I said.

That threw her.

"It's - okay," she said.

That hurt a little. I thought my hair was perfect.

"They made it," I said pointing at the frozen swarm. "After ten generations, they're so small you can't even see them!"

She eyed me suspiciously and came closer. The bunnies were still in her arms, so she set down the rack of car seats. When she got close, she reached up and cautiously touched my hair and then combed her fingers through it. I involuntarily closed my eyes. She stopped and stepped back.

"You enjoyed that," she said surprised.

"I did."

"So, you're not a robot anymore?"

"Oh, I'm still me. I'm metal underneath. I just have a new squishy exterior. It's not real skin, and I don't have any blood or any of that, but it's pretty good, right!"

She pulled at the top of my overalls, peered inside and frowned.

"It's a work-in-progress," I said.

She gave the overalls a couple of quick tugs and stepped back. "I see you're still rockin' the striped look."

I think she disapproved. I waved at the floor behind her, and the activity resumed.

"It's a classic," I said, "and I like the pockets."

"So, it's the future now, right?" she said changing the subject.

I lifted the end of the Stasis-Pod and returned it upright on the floor.

"A little bit, yeah, 1983."

"Who's the president now?"

"It's only been a year, Angel - so - same guy. You don't even know do you?"

"I'm not into politics, Martin."

"Politics is not a *hobby*, Angel. You really have to pay more attention to these things."

"Do I?"

"No," I laughed, "*same circus different monkeys*. Technology is what changes the world. Politics doesn't change the world; it just shakes it back and forth. But it sounded good when I said it, right?"

"Very moving."

"Come on," I said, "I want to go to town and see if my face is good enough. I hope somebody says *you've got a lot of nerve showing your face in this town again*. That would be funny. You know, because that's what I want to do - show my face."

I was hoping for a smile or a laugh, but I got her usual stony expression.

"Yes, I'm sure somebody will say *exactly* that," she said.

We loaded the bunnies in the van which I had cleaned several times while Angel was in the Stasis-Pod. It was show-quality clean. I even repainted the exterior white over baby blue just like the one in *Lost*. I really hoped she wouldn't crash this one. *If wishes wore horses, beggars would hide.*

She told me to play some music, so I sent 'Cadillac Ranch' blasting through the van's speakers.

"Not so loud, Martin! You'll hurt their ears."

I thought their ears were indestructible after the lawn mower incident, but I turned it down anyway.

"Next," she said, and I switched songs.

"Play something I haven't heard before."

"Um, now don't get mad," I said, "but I - had to delete some data to make room for other things."

"Delete?" she said confused.

I don't think she had ever heard that word before.

"It means to throw away, remove, trash. *Erase* is probably the closest word since I'm writing over it."

"You threw away all my music!" she looked horrified.

"No, not *all* of it. Just the stuff I haven't played - and a few movies but just the black and white ones. I know you don't like those."

At that point, music was one of the few good things in her life.

"Look at it this way," I said, "we have something to look forward to."

She pouted as we drove into town. I wanted to see the waterfall, such as it was. Yes, I was wrong about Iowa Falls not having one. The town was named after a natural drop of a few feet, but they dammed it up to try and control the yearly floods. It had rained recently, and I thought we might get a nice view from the bottom of the spillway. It didn't disappoint. Now, some people prefer the random white torrents of natural waterfalls as they tumble over a rocky cliff, but not me. I loved the perfection of the smooth silver sheet arcing over the straight edge.

"She's gone, isn't she," Angel said slowly stroking one of the bunnies and staring at the hypnotic water.

"Yes," I said softly, "but you're not alone."

Nanna had died six months earlier, while Angel was in the pod. I was afraid if I let her out, she would risk certain death to get to the funeral.

"And everybody thinks I'm dead."

"Yes."

We stood there for another half an hour before Angel spoke again.

"Is there any bunny chow at home?"

"Too old. Threw it out," I said. There was something about the falls that made me truncate my sentences. I felt like Jack Webb.

What Angel was referring to was actually called *Purina Rabbit Chow*. Yeah. It was a real thing. They didn't carry it at the grocery store, but since we were in Middle America, *of course,* there was a feed store, and *of course,* they carried crazy animal/pet food of every kind. The guy at the store said they could get food for everything from llamas to monkeys. All the food in the kitchen had also gone bad, so we went for groceries after the feed store. I suggested she leave the rabbits in the van, but she insisted on taking them in and sat the four of them in their side-by-side miniature car seats right there in the shopping cart's baby seat. Never go shopping while hungry. *Everything* looks good. She filled the cart to the brim, and I did my best to put things back on the shelf when she wasn't looking. At the counter, the guy in front of us threw a big fit and stormed out. The cashier wouldn't accept his check or something.

"What's his problem?" Angel asked.

"Oh don't mind him," the cashier said as she tapped the prices into the register. "He lost his job last month, and he blames the whole world for it. Everybody knows it's all that *sumbitch* Reagan's fault."

Angel spun around to me and shouted, "Ronald Reagan!"

"She told you, so it doesn't count," I said examining the ingredients of a Snickers bar.

The cashier eyed us curiously but kept tapping away. I wondered how she could do it all without even looking at the keys, and who would ever know if she got something wrong.

"Anyway," she continued while tapping away at the register and sliding the items down the counter, "that's no excuse. Profanity isn't about being polite it's about control. Everybody *wants* to swear. It's a display of self-control *not* to say it out loud."

This lady seemed to have a handle on things, so I asked her, "what exactly is the difference between a Mountain Lion, a Panther, a Puma, and a Cougar?"

I had deleted those files, and this had been bothering me for weeks. I may have been overestimating the value of the data, but it was like *a scratch I couldn't itch.*

I guess it was a strange question because the cashier lady stopped tapping on the keys, and looked up at me and then Angel.

"You look familiar. Yeah, weren't you making a movie out there at the haunted house last year?"

She looked at me closer, "You look like a movie star. What's your name?"

"I'm Brad Pitt," I said, "but I'm not famous yet."

"Well, with a face like that it won't be long, hon."

I was beaming. Angel informed me that tipping the cashier wasn't the correct grocery store protocol. Her exact words were, "perfectly good money wasted." But I think she earned it.

Angel secured the bunnies in the back seat and helped me get the brown paper bags into the back of the van. They were rectangular and fit snuggly next to each other with no wasted gaps. I loved that. Goddamn OCD.

"What was all that about mountain lions?" Angel asked me as I closed the back hatch.

I sighed, "well, I needed some extra space - up here." I tapped my temple. "So, like I said, I had to delete some things."

After we got in, I continued, "I deleted things I didn't think I would ever need and even some of the RSD data."

"You said that before, what is that?" she asked.

"It's the detailed scan of the earth down to about two feet. It's how I know where all the lost money is."

"You threw away our treasure map!"

"No, I didn't - hey that's a great name for it. I should've thought of that. Huh. No, I didn't delete it all, but now it looks like nobody in China has ever lost or buried anything."

"Oh. Well, just don't throw away any place I might actually go," she said as she backed out of the parking space.

We passed the local library, and I made Angel turn around so I could check it out. She complained about the ice cream, but I wanted to look something up, and without the internet, this was as good as it was going to get. So many books! They smelled old but in a good way - clean and dry. I spotted a lady at the counter and went over. She was just moving books from one pile to another, so I didn't mind interrupting her.

"Can I help you?" she asked.

"Yes!" I said enthusiastically, "can you tell me the difference between a Tamarin and a Marmoset? Tell me everything."

I leaned in for the answer.

"Tamarins are bigger, Marmosets are cuter," she said as if were the most obvious thing in the world.

Someone in the office behind her shouted, "that's a matter of opinion!"

She shushed him over her shoulder. "Are you looking for a book on mammals?" she asked.

"Yes," I said firmly. "I have one hundred forty-two things I need to know, and you probably don't know all of them."

She lifted a single eyebrow. I decided I was going to have to learn to do that.

"Back corner," she pointed, "second stack from the wall."

"Ice cream," Angel said in a high-pitched voice and shifted the bunnies to her other hip.

"If you have a card you can take it home," the lady suggested.

"I can take any of these?" I said waving my hands around, "*all* of these?"

"That's how it works," she said and looked at Angel for some clue about me.

"I want them *all*," I said.

An expression of recognition came over her face, and she began speaking slower and nodding her head. "You can have all of them," she said and held up one finger. "but you'll need a place to keep them - and someone to take care of them. I'll keep them here for you, and you can come back anytime you want, okay?"

"Deal!" I shouted and ran to the back of the room.

I found a book called 'Mammals of the World' and darted back to the counter where Angel and the librarian were filling out a card. As we left, she looked at Angel and said, "you're doing such a wonderful thing!"

"What was *that* about?" I asked when we got back in the van.

"She thinks you're mentally challenged, and I didn't disabuse her of it," Angel said. "I told her I was your sister, and that I'm going to devote my life to taking care of you."

Her correct use of the word *disabuse* impressed and surprised me. I wondered what Angel was like as a ten-year-old. Was she a nerdy girl?

"The librarian said that? Seriously?" I said. "Well, she's in for a shock when I tell her I'm a super-intelligent robot from the future." I started to get out of the van.

"Not right now, the ice cream is already soft."

"Ice cream - ice cream! What's the big deal with ice cream? Hey, that gives me an idea for my next upgrade! How do you feel about another nap?"

"I just bought groceries, Martin. I'd like to stay awake long enough to eat them."

～

CHAPTER SUMMARY

Here's where we are so far:

Angel has traveled from 1982 into the distant future of 1983. Martin has shown Angel his swarm of tiny robots, and she has given him a scalp massage. Angel has learned that Nanna has died. A waterfall has mesmerized them both. Angel has refilled the refrigerator, and Martin owns the contents of a library.

MARTIN VERSION 5

"I changed the start-up sequence," I said. "It's more gradual now. The desire to bash your head against jagged metal should be reduced to a manageable level."

"Charming," she said.

We were in the basement getting ready for the next jump into the future. I didn't think Angel would stand for another solo trip, so I was going along this time.

"Do you want to be sedated?" I asked and started playing the appropriate song from *The Ramones.*

She bit her lower lip and thought about it, "whiskey?"

"Fresh out," I said.

"Heck with it," she said, "I'll take it sober."

I was stunned at her self-control and also the use of the word *heck.* Just a week before, she would have used an F-bomb and probably another as a modifier.

"Heck?" I said sarcastically.

"I'm quitting for the kids," she said *not* sarcastically.

"They're just bunnies, Angel. They need to be set loose in the woods anyway."

"Stop trying to come between me and my kids," she said slowly through gritted teeth.

"Okay, let's set that aside for the time being," I said and glanced around for the shotgun. "The Stasis-Pod has a Temporal Fuse now just like the van, so if we're about to snooze through something important, it'll wake us up early. Any questions?"

"Yeah, you're really coming this time instead of just lying and drugging me?"

"Yes, Angel. I'm going. Promise. Any other questions?" I asked.

"How far are we going?"

"Two years," I said. "Thomas will be popping in from the future at the farm north of here. It's just a guess, but I think we're supposed to do something there."

I set the timer, and it began beeping its countdown.

"After you," I said motioning to the Stasis-Pod which was standing upright for this trip.

"No, *you* first. I don't trust you, Martin."

"We only have five seconds left," I said, but she refused to move, so I jumped in quickly and pulled her in behind me. It was a tight fit especially with those stupid rabbits and their rack of car seats. She closed the door just in time. There was a flash of light, a sharp jolt, and the door popped open.

"Great," she said disappointed and got out. "Let me know when it's actually working…"

I looked at the wall clock that I had modified to show the date, and it said 1985.

"Hey, it worked!" I said. "I mean, I knew it would, but experiencing it first hand was - wow! *Fast!*"

I noticed Angel staring at something behind the machine. I turned to see a naked man standing in the corner surrounded by a large pile of dust.

"It's done!" I shouted and hurried over to inspect it.

"It?" she said hugging her rabbits tighter.

"Yeah, it's my new body. Version four - or five, depending on how you count. The tiny robots worked on it while we were away. I can eat and drink now!"

"And other things too, I see," she said glancing down.

"Oh yeah, that. Well, if I'm going to eat and drink, I need to dispose of it all somehow, so I thought what the heck - for authenticity if nothing else. What do you think?" I was pretty excited and had already started copying my brain to it.

"It's a little creepy the way it just stands there," she said.

I got enough of myself copied over and raised my arms in my new body. "Is this better? Tada!"

She jumped back, "is that you, Martin?"

"It is," I said from both the new and old bodies. "I'm actually in both places while I finish moving."

"Moving? You can't stay in both?"

"No, I'm deleting as I go to avoid the awkwardness of convincing the old-me to kill himself."

"So you're still metal under there?" she asked pointing at the new-me.

"Yep. I'm just like *Da Terminatah*!" I said. "But, less murdery."

"What are you going to do with - old-you?" she asked.

I went over, opened its chest, and removed the Babbage Unit.

"I'll keep the old one and turn it back into the spiderbot configuration. Eight extra hands might be useful. I wish I'd had it before I deleted all that trivia. Without the internet to look things up, the list of unimportant questions is building to a critical mass. I may have to do a sleep-over in the library."

"So no more Dirk Pitt?" she asked looking at the old me now frozen mid-smile.

"*Brad* Pitt," I corrected. "Nah, it would have been awkward as we head into the nineties. What do you think of *this* face?"

"It's okay. Who are you supposed to be this time?"

"I decided to avoid any celebrities we might actually run into. I'm George Gordon Byron - Lord Byron!"

"That's appropriate," she said. "What was it they said about him? Mad, bad, and dangerous to know? Sounds like you."

Something seriously creepy was going on in her head. I think everything she ever heard or read was now crystal clear in her mind and she had gone from party girl to witty nerd in less than a month.

"Exactly!" I said. "Do I look sinister too? That's what I was going for."

"No, you look like a man-child," she said and stroked my cheek. "Your face is too smooth for sinister. If you want that, you'll need some facial hair."

"Ah! Good idea! Maybe a Van Dyke?" I suggested.

"That's a sinister look all right, but I prefer it like this, pretty boy," she said. "Let's take a drive. I want to see if we can leave yet."

She looked down again and added, "you better put some clothes on."

I started to take the striped overalls off of old-me, and she made a clicking sound of disapproval. The overalls were too small, and the legs only went to mid-calf.

"I'll get around to shopping for different clothes as soon as we have time," I said. "But I need pockets. Lots of pockets, or it's no deal."

∾

CHAPTER SUMMARY

Here's where we are so far:

Martin has gone five minutes without lying to Angel. They have successfully jumped two more years to 1985 while awake, and without bashing their heads against jagged metal. Martin's tiny robots have finished his new body which is capable of passing gas and other useful things.

WONDROUS TREASURES

W e left my workshop through the tunnel to the garage and
Angel opened the roll-up door.

"Who mowed the lawn?" she asked as we got a look at the
property.

"We're supposed to be caretakers Angel. We need to *take care,* at
least a little. I upgraded the mower before we jumped. It's automatic,
but it runs at night to avoid suspicion."

A horrified look came across her face.

"Don't worry," I said, "I added infrared sensors, so it won't run
over anything - at least nothing warm-blooded. I bet there are stories
of a growling monster that prowls the haunted house in the dark of
night. Hey! Remind me to set it to only mow when there's no moon.
Oh! Even better: when there's a *full* moon so they can *see* that it's a
mower being driven by a ghost! Awesome."

Angel didn't roll her eyes, but she blinked extra slowly, which gave
the same effect. She strapped the bunnies in and started the van. I was
impressed that it actually ran after two years without maintenance.
The dust layer made me squirm as I got in and made a mental note to
wash it at the first opportunity. At the gate, Angel stopped and did
something she had never done before. She went to the mailbox and

checked inside. I had deleted all information regarding mailboxes except what they looked like, and I was very curious when she retrieved a small cardboard box from it.

"What is it?" I asked barely concealing my excitement.

Seeing my interest, she got into the van very slowly and took glee in taking as much time as she could in fastening her seatbelt before opening the box in glacially slow movements. Once the end was open, she dumped the contents onto her lap. It was four brightly colored collars. Each had a tiny silver tag. Angel handed them to me. The names on the tags were Terry, Francis, Robin, and Chris.

"Are these for the *rabbits*?" I asked finally getting it.

"I can't tell the boys from the girls," she said, "and it seems rude to go poking around down there, so I picked names that work for both."

"Who put them in the mailbox? What's going on?"

She looked at me as if I had two heads.

"The - *mailman*," she said sarcastically. "Nobody in town could do the engraving, so I used mail order. There was an ad in the back of a magazine."

"Someone *made* these for you," I said trying to understand, "and brought them here to you?"

"Yeah - duh. That's how it works, Martin."

"Jesus, I've been making everything myself - from scratch. I didn't know this existed. Shit."

"Relax, Martin," she said, "I don't think you would have been able to find a mail-order time machine or humanoid robot body."

We couldn't leave until she gave each rabbit his/her collar and told him/her what his/her name was followed by a kiss on the forehead. When she finally got us back on the road, we tried each direction out of town with no luck. The van stalled every time.

"I don't understand," I said. "Thomas is due to arrive in thirty-six hours."

"Try again tomorrow?" she asked.

"I guess so. I can't think of anything else to try."

"Get out the map. I want to find some treasure," she said.

"If you *need* something, I can have the tiny robots make pretty much anything non-biological," I offered.

"No, I don't need the money. I just want to have some fun and find something shiny."

I don't need the money? I couldn't believe what I had heard.

"Well, okay. Gold or silver?"

She giggled and rubbed her hands together, "surprise me!"

I directed her to the local school. She parked the van, and we went around to the back playground where all the swings dangled empty in the breeze. It was summer, so there wasn't a kid in sight.

"Here? There's a treasure *here?*" she said.

"Treasure might be overstating it," I said, "and it's over there." I pointed to the tall weeds beyond the edge of the playground.

She set the rabbits down and released them from their car seats. They hopped around a little in the short grass but didn't seem inclined to go any farther as we ventured into the weeds. About thirty feet in, I stopped and said, "it's somewhere in this area," and swept my foot across the ground. I knew exactly where it was, but I thought she'd have more fun if it took a while. She dropped down on all fours and began probing the ground.

"Is it buried?"

I could already see it, but my vision was better than hers.

"No, I don't think it's buried. Maybe an animal moved it around. You should widen your search."

She crawled off in the wrong direction.

"Perhaps *this* direction," I said.

She looked up at me, and I was caught.

"Are you messing with me, Martin? Do you see it?"

I laughed, and she stood up irritated. I bent to pick it up. It was a silver bracelet with several oddly shaped things dangling from it. The weather hadn't been kind to it, so it was more black than shiny in places.

"I'll need to clean and polish it," I said as I handed it to her.

She put it on and examined each of the charms, "I love it!" she squealed and hugged me, which, I have to admit, felt pretty good. It also got me wondering about the nature of our relationship. I was okay with things as they were, but I had read up on the subject and suspected she was probably not. Or, at least, she would be getting restless soon, and that might bring trouble.

"Hungry yet?" I said. "Groceries seem to be a waste of money for us. How about the diner. I want to try some ice cream."

"Yeah let's go," she said, and we returned to the van, retrieving the rabbits on the way. I was hoping they had run off, but they didn't seem interested in freedom.

Angel let me drive, and I was pretty good at it, but I tended to hop the curbs on right turns. We arrived at the diner between the lunch and dinner crowds, so the place was almost empty. I wanted to sit at the counter, but there was no place to hide the rabbits. We got a booth instead and slipped them under the table. I think the waitress saw but didn't complain. Angel's reputation may have preceded her. *Don't mess with the crazy rabbit lady.* I ordered plain vanilla ice cream. Angel suggested chocolate or at least walnuts and whipped cream, but I wanted the unadorned experience. I was pleased to see she ordered a salad with her steak and potatoes, but then I saw she was just slipping bits of lettuce to the bunnies as she ate the rest. The ice cream was cold, had a pleasant texture, and I recognized the high sugar content. I can't say I *enjoyed* it, but it was a good baseline for comparing other foods. Sitting there with Angel felt good, and eating was part of it, so that's probably why I play that memory in my head more than any other since then.

Angel left a tip that was way too small, so I dropped an extra twenty to the table when she wasn't looking. We went to the dam to see the spillway again, but it wasn't flowing much this time. I guess it hadn't rained lately. This little town was growing on me. Don't get me wrong, after the novel beauty of the first snow wears off, it's pretty much a frozen wasteland in Winter, and Spring is a horror show of floods and mud, but Summer and Fall are actually quite lovely.

"What now?" I asked as we got back into the van. "More treasure?"

"Yes!" she growled. "I'm in!"

"Okay, I know just the thing," I said and added in a lower tone, "but it'll be dangerous."

"Oh, now I'm *really* in. Where is it?" she asked.

I directed her to the western edge of town where we had been many times testing the limits of whatever was keeping us there. The Temporal Fuse tripped, and the van slowed to a stop just as it had every other time on that stretch of road. Angel was about to hit the red button on the dash and turn around when I stopped her.

"See that barn on the left?"

I pointed to the road ahead of us about a quarter of a mile. It was a solitary building, and the road was very curvy, so there wasn't a neighbor in sight.

"There used to be a house, but I guess it fell down. There's a very nice treasure in what used to be the backyard."

"So, that's what you meant by danger. It's outside of town," she said.

"Exactly. Still up for it?"

She chewed her lower lip and thought about it for a bit.

"You can leave the bunnies in the car," I said, "they'll be fine."

It was getting cloudy, and they were in no danger of overheating, so she agreed. I pushed the van to the side of the road, and we jumped the barbed wire fence. As we crossed the small pasture, I kept looking around for the bull that I was sure was about to charge us, but nothing dangerous showed up. If Angel was nervous, she didn't show it. We climbed over the fence at the other end of the field and stopped to look at the barn. It was very old and very gray, but at least it wasn't leaning like so many in the area were.

"Are you ready?" I said just as a lightning strike, less than a mile away, made a bright flash accompanied by a simultaneous boom that I could feel in my chest. I didn't have an amygdala, so I didn't flinch, but Angel almost jumped out of her skin.

"It's over there," I said quickly dropping any pretense of ignorance and pointed to a spot on the ground.

We rushed over, and I picked up a gold ring with four small stones of various colors. She recognized the mother's ring with four birthstones for what it was, and I thought she was going to cry, but then the clouds opened up, and it started pouring. We ran to the barn, but even so, our clothes were soaked by the time we got inside. I was impressed that the roof was in such good condition. This thing even had a wooden floor. It was dark everywhere but near the open door so Angel stopped there to get a better look at the ring. She slipped it on and turned to hug me again, and this time I kissed her. I half expected her to recoil in horror. Instead, she pulled off her shirt and tossed it over a wooden railing to dry.

"Let's get out of these wet clothes, Martin. It's time to show me if *everything* works."

~

CHAPTER SUMMARY

Here's where we are so far:

The lawn has been mowed by an invisible midnight lawn mowerist. Martin has learned about the fascinating world of mail order. The rabbits now have jewelry and confused gender roles. Angel and Martin have found some treasure. Martin has tasted ice-cream and other things.

THAT GIN BLOSSOMS SONG

I made Angel breakfast the next morning, and she shocked me by actually getting out of bed even though it was barely sunrise. I think she was anxious to see if we could finally leave town. Thomas was due to drop out of the sky sometime after noon. She squealed with delight when she saw what I had done with the bracelet and ring. It was just a cleaning really, but they looked brand new.

The rabbits were eating tiny carrots from a plastic bag. I wondered where they grew carrots that small and if tiny children with tiny fingers plucked them out of the ground. Once the bunnies had their breakfast, Angel sat down, and I served her the usual huge amount of bacon and eggs.

"I can't eat this much, Martin," she said.

Now, she had eaten *at least* that much every morning since I gave her the injection, but somehow, she was now shocked at the pound of bacon and half-dozen scrambled eggs. I guess whatever transformation had been going on inside her was over and she was back to normal caloric requirements.

"You try some," she said and got another plate from the cupboard.

I tried the bacon, but the eggs are a bad smell, so I passed on them. I even tried one of the carrots. I have to say, none of it tasted as good as the ice cream. Angel finished about a fourth of what I gave her and went to get dressed.

It looked like another stormy day when we finally got on the road *several hours later.* The van died at the edge of town just as it had the day before.

"This can't be right," I said and pressed the reset button. "Go a little farther."

I motioned to the stretch of dirt road that led north toward the Murphy Farm. She looked a little worried and glanced back at the rabbits but eased the van forward. It tripped again. This time I hit the button with my fist. Before we started moving again, a lightning bolt struck a tree so close to us I thought the windows would shatter.

"Nope. Nope. Nope." Angel said and twisted around to steer the van in reverse.

She got all the way back to the crossroad, and we stopped to think.

"What the hell are we here for if it's not the Murphy Farm? It's only five miles away!" I was more frustrated than I had ever been.

"Relax, Martin. We'll just try again tomorrow," she said, "but send your queen bee. I want to see a time-machine-slash-space-ship land."

"Angel, I told you before. It's not a queen…" I looked over at her, and she was smiling. "Okay, I'll send *the drone.* Let's hope it doesn't get struck by lightning."

I sent a transmission back to the mansion, and the drone came to life. The basement door unlocked and opened enough for it to fly up the stairs and into the empty first floor. As it cleared one of the window openings, I announced, "launching forward recon drone number seven!"

"Wait, how many of those things do you *have?*" Angel asked.

"Just one," I said, "but it sounds cooler if you say it like that."

I opened the glove compartment, took out a pair of binoculars and handed them to Angel. She took them and looked at me curiously.

"What are these for? The farm's *miles* away,"

"I modified them to show the image from the drone's spherical camera. Point them in any direction, and you see the view it captures from that direction."

Angel put them to her eyes and giggled, "Co-ol."

She started craning her neck to see every direction before taking them away from her eyes to pass them to me.

"Oh, I don't need them. I have implants. I can see the same thing without help. Those are for you."

"Nice, Martin! Thanks!" and she leaned over and kissed me before returning the binoculars to her eyes. "I feel like a *spy*!"

We watched as the rooftops of downtown sped beneath the drone on its way toward us.

"Here it comes. Wave!" I said, and we thrust our arms out of the windows as it passed overhead.

"Wow that's faster than before," she said.

"I made some improvements. It still won't do Mach-one because of the aerodynamics, but it can get close."

It made it to the edge of the Murphy farm, and we could see Brad on his tractor. It was too early for Thomas to show up, so I dropped the drone down just inside the line of trees to wait. We got a grasshopper's-eye view of the sky as huge-looking weeds swayed in front of the camera-ball. I have a low threshold for boredom, and my focus drifted to other things while we waited.

Thomas lowered into frame, and that snapped my attention back to the video feed.

"Angel! Angel! He's here!" I shouted.

She had fallen asleep, but now we were both focused on the show. Brad was on his tractor at the far edge of the frame and a sixty-foot silver sphere lowered to within three feet of the ground. It hovered for a second before dropping violently to the soft dirt. There must have been a slight grade because he also rolled about ten degrees before stopping. Brad jumped off the tractor and started jogging across the field toward Thomas.

"That's Brad," I said to Angel.

I didn't think she heard me.

"He's a farmer," I added.

"Duh," she said.

We watched as Brad cautiously approached Thomas.

"Turn the knob on top to zoom in if you want a closer look," I said to Angel and showed her where it was.

As Brad slowly circled the ship, the gangway ramp rotated open automatically and came to rest on the ground.

"He's probably terrified," I said.

"He doesn't *look* terrified," Angel said, "he looks curious."

I decided to add some dramatic commentary, "M is inside, injured and unconscious. Brad is conflicted…"

"He doesn't look conflicted either," she interrupted.

"…on the one hand," I continued, "he's *terrified* of what must obviously be an alien spacecraft…"

Angel snorted, "oh, please. Wait, is Thomas *really* an alien spacecraft?"

"No, Angel. He's not an *alien* spacecraft. He's an *annoying* spacecraft who abuses his robots, but he was made right here on Earth by the Committees. He's *supposed* to be surveying asteroids, but from what I observed during my time with him, he didn't seem too concerned with doing any of that."

Brad came around to the opening and looked up the ramp, and I continued my commentary, "…he peeks inside the *alien abode*, unsure what to do next," I said.

Angel growled at that.

Brad spotted M's unconscious body on the floor, and he sprinted up the ramp. "He sees a poor defenseless woman and decides to abduct her. Who knows what fate awaits her as he spirits her away to his secret lair where…"

"Good God, Martin!" Angel said. "He saw she was hurt and ran right in to help her!"

"All right, maybe that was a little harsh," I admitted.

We saw Brad emerge carrying M, and he jogged off toward the farmhouse.

"He's pretty strong too," Angel said craning her neck forward for absolutely no reason.

"Yeah, yeah, he's strong as an ox and twice as smart," I said.

I turned to see Angel smiling at me.

"What?"

"You're jealous," she said.

Holy crap. She was right. I *was* jealous. How could *that* be? I wondered what Thomas had done to me to cause this nonsense.

"Please," I said, "I'm a super-intelligent robot from the future. What's he?"

She returned the binoculars to her eyes, "tall, muscular, brave, strong, caring…"

"Iowa farm boy," I said derisively.

"…who's also tall, muscular, brave, strong and caring," she finished.

"There's no comparison," I managed to get out, "and I don't get jealous!"

She laughed out loud at that, and I made a mental note to add more muscles on my next upgrade. Lord Byron had a pretty face, but I don't think he got to the gym very often.

~

CHAPTER SUMMARY

Here's where we are so far:

Thomas, an intelligent spaceship from the future, has dropped-and-rolled without being on fire. A queen bee has shown Angel a farmer and Martin has discovered jealousy.

A WITCH WITH NICE HARE

I knew nothing much would happen up at the Murphy farm for a while, so we went home, stopping off for a few non-perishables at the grocery store on the way. The next morning, we tried all the exits out of town again to no avail. I left the drone in the field so we could watch what was going on up there.

"They'll repair Thomas," I said pacing the kitchen while Angel ate breakfast food for dinner, "and he'll leave and go back to the future in a couple of days."

"Maybe we're supposed to do something *after* he leaves," she said poking a fork at her scrambled eggs.

"Maybe," I said unconvinced. "I don't know what that would *be*. Nothing happens here after that. The committees turn the farm into a spaceport, but that's not for several decades," I laughed, "and by then, nobody even lives out here, so there's no reason at all to - that's it! It has to be. We're supposed to make sure the committees build the spaceport way the hell out here in the middle of nowhere!"

"Okay, why would anybody build a spaceport in Iowa?" she asked.

"That's just it! They wouldn't, but it has to be done. It's why Thomas's automated systems brought him here. If they don't build the spaceport here, he won't come here. He and M won't meet the

Murphys, and that changes things a lot. They're the reason I was dropped off in 1982. That has to be it. We should check the edge of town every day just to be sure. But I really think the spaceport thing with the committees is what we need to do. Then we'll be free to go anywhere we want and do anything we want. We'll get in the Stasis-Pod again and set it for 2020. If there's something between now and then, the Temporal Fuse will trip and wake us up early."

"Sounds like a plan," Angel said. "I just have one question. Which committee decides where to build spaceports? Isn't that a NASA thing?"

"No it's not *A committee* it's *The Committees.* They run everything in the future because humanity is too busy playing beer pong to get anything done. I think if we get a request in early we can steer them in the right direction."

"And they're not human? They're like you?"

"What? No. Nobody's like me. I'm unique, erudite, flexible, and affable - neither famous nor infamous, neither flammable nor inflammable..."

Angel checked her watch.

"...anyway, what was I saying?"

"I don't know. I stopped listening after erudite."

I struggled to remember.

"The Committees," she said and carved donuts of impatience in the air with her hand.

"Oh right. The Committees are just artificial intelligences without bodies. They just sort of float around in computer networks and try to bore each other to death with endless meetings."

"Ghosts in the machine," she said seriously.

"Huh," I said, "yeah, I guess they *are.*"

The next day we tested the city limits again without luck even though Angel rubbed several rabbits' feet. Two days later we watched from the kitchen table as version one of my spiderbot body emerged from Thomas.

"Aren't you cute!" Angel exclaimed, "Look how small you were!"

"Yeah," I said, "that's the standard size model. Thomas made me a plus-size body before he ditched me in 1982."

As the previous version of me led the way into the farmhouse, I filled Angel in on what they were doing. "Thomas is telling them how he was damaged, and that he can fix all their medical problems. Mostly he's just bragging about how awesome he is. They'll agree to go with him and try to save the world or some nonsense."

We tried a few more times to get closer to Thomas but failed. The next day we watched as they all boarded the spherical ship and disappeared into the clouds, and it was all over.

"Well that was a bust," I complained to Angel. "I guess we should get back in the Stasis-Pod and see how far we can get. Any objection?"

"Not from me," she said. "Let's go."

We packed up the bunnies and went through the tunnel to the basement. The keypad beeped as I tapped in 2020 on the Stasis-Pod control. We got in without any fanfare. It was almost becoming routine. A second later when we emerged, the clock said 2006.

"Something woke us up early," I said looking around the room.

"So it's *the year* two thousand and six," Angel said in awe and then shrugged. "Looks pretty much the same."

She set the rabbits down on the table and swiped a finger across the thick layer of dust.

"…just dirtier," she added.

"Angel, please," I said, "it's taking all the self-control I can muster to not start cleaning everything. Please don't talk about how filthy everything is or I'll lose control, and we'll never find out why we're here."

"I'm just saying, twenty-one years is a lot of dust," she said.

"Okay, that's it," I said. "I'm going to clean the vacuum, then I'm going to use it to clean everything else, and then I'm going to clean the vacuum again. Your job during all this is to whisper in my ear like the slave to Caesar *You are not crazy. You are not crazy.*"

That got a giggle, but I was only half kidding. We took a quick inventory of the room, and nothing had changed. I took a not-very-detailed look at twenty-one years of security camera footage and, apart from some boys trying - and failing - to spend the night in the *haunted* house, nothing really happened. The tiny robots had kept up the maintenance of the self-driving lawn mower, and it had kept up with minimal *care-takering*, so I guessed we weren't evicted yet.

"Let's check the apartment," I said and opened the door to the tunnel.

I really just wanted to see if the van would start. It didn't. I forgot to have the robots keep it in good shape. The tires had gone flat, and the battery was dead, but an hour later we were on the road to town. Even after inflating them, the tires were now only round-*ish* because of the flat spots, and they shook the van as we rolled down the street. We decided to stop at the diner first, and Angel parked in front. It was mid-morning on a Saturday, so there was a good crowd. The bell above the glass door jingled as we entered and everyone in the place stopped to turn and gape at us. A hush fell over the room as we sat down at the only available booth. Angel cautiously slid the rabbit-filled rack of tiny car seats under the table. I expected the conversations to resume at some point, but they didn't. Eventually, the waitress approached and handed us menus with shaking hands. Angel and I exchanged glances as she backed away.

"What's going on," she whispered.

"No clue," I whispered back.

They were all still staring at us when a young couple paid quickly and left in a rush. That broke the spell, and everyone else did the same. The waitress had retreated to the kitchen, leaving us alone in the dining area.

"Are you hungry?" I asked Angel.

"Not particularly," she said, and we stood quickly to leave.

Curiosity had kept the fleeing patrons hanging around across the street and milling around in the side parking lot. I distinctly heard the word *Witch* as I opened the door, but they all fell silent again to watch us leave. Angel was pretty calm through all this. If she ever cared what other people thought of her, it was hidden well. The tires made more thumping noises as we returned to the mansion to figure out what was going on. Angel parked in the garage, and I saw movement at the far edge of the property. The camera there showed me three boys on bicycles pedaling madly in our direction.

"Close the door," I said, and Angel hit the button on the remote. The overhead door screamed its way down, and I made a mental note to oil *everything*.

Before Angel got out of the van, I handed her the binoculars and her Bluetooth earbuds. She looked puzzled.

"We have visitors," I said. "We may get this figured out if they get within range of the microphones on my cameras."

I fed the view from the front gate to her binoculars, and she saw the boys approach. They *intentionally* stirred up as much dust as possible coming to a stop.

"Why would they do that?" I asked. "No wonder there's so much dust everywhere."

Angel lowered the binoculars from her eyes, "Martin, it's not their fault the world is dirty," she said.

They were staring at the main house through the wrought iron bars of the gate.

"It's true," one of them said in a solemn tone.

"Just ghost stories," another said and added, "complete bullshit."

"Not ghosts. Witches," the first one said, "it's all in the book."

Angel looked at me and mouthed *what book?*

"Witches?" the second boy pressed. "You mean there's more than one?"

"Maybe," he replied. "They can take the form of rabbits, and you saw how many they had right? That proves it."

"What about the man? Is he a witch too?"

"Not a witch - a *homunculus*. The book says she might create a man from a rabbit, but he'll be stupid because he's still only got a rabbit's brain. You saw how he was dressed. That proves it."

Angel lowered the binoculars and shot daggers at me.

"This is not my fault," I said. "My clothing choice is irrelevant. I think that fact that we disappear for years at a time and never age *might* have something to do with it. Also, the rabbits don't help. Just saying - you might as well have a black cat and a broom."

She returned the binoculars to her eyes as the first boy, who seemed to be the leader of their little gang reached the crescendo of the story.

"Witches are old and ugly," one of the other boys argued. "No way she's a witch. She's beautiful."

Angel chuckled and looked smug.

"That's just Hollywood nonsense," the leader deflected. "The book says *the witch doesn't age*. She can also take the form of a rabbit and *disappear* at will. Then she reappears behind you," he clapped his hands together for effect, "*and you're caught!*"

"What do you think she would do to you?" one of the others asked in a meek voice.

"I don't know," the leader said, "probably turn you into another idiot in ridiculous clothes."

I couldn't take any more of this and headed for the rear door of the garage.

"Where are you going?" Angel said.

"I've had enough of this nonsense. I'm going down there and set them straight."

"...the Rabbit Witch sleeps in the mansion, and the homunculus rabbit-man sleeps above the garage," he continued as I came around the corner of the building.

"That's completely inaccurate," I shouted down to them, "she sleeps above the garage! I don't actually sleep *anywhere!*"

It was important to me to clear this up, but they were gone by the time I reached the gate. They stirred up more dust, too.

～

CHAPTER SUMMARY

Here's where we are so far:

Martin and Angel have skipped to 2006. The good townsfolk are searching their basements for torches and pitchforks. Martin has vowed to update his wardrobe someday, and several children have ridden bicycles.

THE WITCHING HOUR

Angel didn't want to go back into town, so I made my first attempt at making edible food with the robots. I set a charcoal briquette on the kitchen table and dripped some water on it. A cloud of gray fog flew over to envelop it. The black lump looked like it was dissolving, and in its place, were tiny whitish doughnut shapes.

"Cheerios?" Angel asked.

"Yeah, they're pretty simple," I said. "Try one."

She wrinkled her nose but cautiously chose one and sniffed at it.

"Smells right," she said.

I wondered if she could even smell a single Cheerio.

"It's identical to the store-bought version," I said. "Go ahead, taste it."

She popped it in her mouth and chewed slowly.

"It's a little dry," she said.

"Well, I don't think I can make milk. That would be a moon-landing. This is Sputnik."

I got a bowl from the cupboard and scooped up the Cheerios for her. She took the bowl and retreated to the living room to watch TV while I made more for the rabbits. After she had gone to bed, I went through the tunnel to the basement so I could work on trying to make sugar. I wanted to surprise Angel with FrootLoops in the morning. My previous body was completely back to its original spiderbot configuration. He wasn't much for conversation, but eight extra hands were a great help.

At around midnight the security camera picked up some motion at the front gate. One of the kids from earlier was back. I watched as he carelessly tossed his bike to the ground without even trying to use the kickstand. He threw a home-made rope ladder onto the wrought iron gate. After a few more attempts, he got it to catch on the upper edge and climbed up. On each side of the gate, there were square pillars made of brick, so he was able to rest on the flat top while he pulled the ladder up. I made a mental note to do something about that. *The Nazis used broken bottles on the wall around the Warsaw Ghetto. Something like that would keep these kids off. Angel probably wouldn't go for it, though. Maybe if I leave off the part about Nazis. Nah, she'll still veto it. Maybe I could just add a rounded concrete top that you can't sit on...*

My attention snapped back as he jumped off the ladder inside the yard. He looked around cautiously. I bet he was wondering where the growling monster was. Before I could get the mower started, he ran to the front door and strolled right in. I cursed myself for not checking the lock earlier and then remembered the gaping window-holes and decided the front door lock was security-theater at best. There were a few cameras inside, so I could see what he was doing. He turned on a flashlight. *This kid came prepared.* He went to the bottom of the wide staircase. He stood there for a while examining the steps. They were made of solid oak but all the years in the elements had taken its toll. They were in terrible shape, and he decided not to press his luck. Instead, he swept the light across the enormous room and stopped when something caught his eye. It was just a reflection in the puddle of water that had pooled up in the center of the sagging floor. He went to investigate. As he approached it, the support beams groaned - and collapsed. The pillars holding up the second story and the rest of the structure held but the center of the room dropped several feet as a hole opened at the bottom of the new parquet funnel that used to be the floor.

I was up and running for the door in a microsecond. His feet slid out from under him, and his head struck the newly inclining surface. The workshop door opened automatically for me as I approached it at full speed. His limp body slid through the hole and dropped to the concrete basement floor with a sickly thud. I slid to a stop and picked him up as gently as I could. The house was groaning as it settled into its bizarre new configuration. I was sure the entire thing was about to collapse on top of us. The closest wall was in the wrong direction, but I needed to stay away from the center, so I ran for it and made my way around the perimeter back to my workshop. As soon as I laid him down on the floor, the door to the tunnel burst open, and Angel stepped in.

"What the hell, Martin!" she said out of breath.

I was kneeling over him, "it's one of the kids from yesterday. He fell through the floor," I said.

"Oh my God," she said as she saw his motionless body, "is he dead?"

It was a bad head injury, and I was sure he wouldn't make it.

"No, he'll be fine," I said.

That calmed her, but not by much. She was still shaking while I brought the spiderbot over and had it scan and probe around.

"Let's get this backpack off," I said and eased him up.

After a few seconds, I announced the prognosis, "His brain is swelling, and there's some damage too."

"Oh my God," she said and started crying, "we have to call an ambulance!"

"Already done, but it's thirty miles away," I said, "and they can't deal with this much trauma. I'll have to try and fix it myself."

She was rapidly stroking his limp hand. I thought she'd leave blisters. The spiderbot retreated, and I brought over the swarm of nanobots. They entered the gash in his scalp, and I was able to stop the bleeding. Repairing the damage was way beyond anything I could do so I improvised and built a small scaffold with some of the tiny robots and just left them in there. They might eventually be able to interface with his brain - or they might not. At that scale, the properties of metal weren't very good, so I had been making them out of organic materials. If the hospital took an X-ray, it wouldn't show anything unusual. The skull fracture wasn't too difficult to repair, and I was done in five minutes. Angel was going through his backpack and came up with a book about witches and a library card.

"It says his name is Kent Cunningham," she said and turned her attention to the book. Several yellow sticky notes protruded from the pages. She turned it around to show me an image of a young woman and several rabbits. She choked out a laugh and had to wipe her nose with her sleeve. "Stupid kid," she said between sniffles.

A loud bang made Angel turn, and she saw the spiderbot disassembling the Stasis-Pod into flat panels.

"What's he doing?" she demanded.

"I was telling the truth about the ambulance, Angel. I have a connection to the phone line at the closest neighbor's house. I've been using it to play with the Internet. Anyway, I used it to call the hospital. I gave them the address and told them a kid was injured in the basement. I think we only have about thirty minutes before they get here, and we need to be gone."

The spiderbot started carting the panels through the tunnel. Angel just looked confused. I snapped my fingers in front of her face.

"Angel! Get the bunnies and anything else you don't want to leave behind. We're not coming back."

The house had stopped groaning, and nothing else had fallen in, so I lifted Kent and carried him back to the spot where he fell. I laid him down as gently as I could before retreating through the workshop and into the tunnel.

"We can't just leave him there," Angel complained as I tried to pull her down the tunnel.

The spiderbot came back for another load, and as he passed us, I had him inject her with a sedative. He finished loading the equipment into the van, and I carried Angel. It took everything I had to fight the urge to release the rabbits in the woods, but I knew Angel would be angry enough about the sedative. I pulled the van out of the garage, and the spiderbot ran down to open the gate. *He's pretty handy to have around*, I thought as he got in the backseat and laid down on the floor. The garage door closed and the property returned to its usual dark gloom. The drone showed me the progress of the ambulance, and I waited a few blocks away to monitor Kent from the cameras in the basement. The hospital must have called the police too because they were right behind them. The cops stayed to look around the place after Kent was loaded up and on his way. I waited until they left, sent the drone back to remove the cameras, and put everything back the way it was before we arrived twenty years earlier. Angel woke up as we were pulling into the driveway of the Murphy farm.

～

CHAPTER SUMMARY

Here's where we are so far:

Martin has made unsweetened cereal. Angel has eaten a lump of charcoal. A boy named Kent has driven the Rabbit Witch from his village. Martin and Angel have managed to get even farther away from civilization.

EDEN IS BURNING

"Where *are* we?" Angel asked as she sat up in bed. "How long have I been asleep?" She pressed the heel of her hand into one eye and then the other. "The last thing I remember is that kid dying on the floor." She stopped her stretching to look at me seriously, and her eyes glistened with tears. "He's not dead, is he?"

"He'll be fine," I said from the bedside chair. I put down the paperback I was thumbing through. "He may have a little OCD and a strange affinity for skeeball but nothing major."

"You saved him? Doesn't that change things? How did we get away with *that?*"

I just shook my head. "I have no idea. There's nothing in my files about a Kent Cunningham. We were able to leave town, so maybe that was what we had to do - save a kid. Or maybe we just had to wait out some clock, and it was a coincidence. Who knows."

"Where are we," she asked again looking around the bedroom. It was all paisley wallpaper and old furniture. It reminded me of her grandmother's house but less cluttered.

"It's the Murphy farm. The county took it a year after they all left with Thomas, but apparently, nobody wanted to buy the place. They probably thought it was cursed because they just disappeared. Or maybe they expected them to come back from wherever they went, and buying the property out from under them would have seemed rude. Anyway, no one's lived here for over twenty years. I made that mattress and pillow for you. The sheets too. You don't want to know what the old stuff looked like. You're welcome by the way. The spiderbot is cleaning the rest of the house. You should stay in here for a while unless you have a strong stomach. It's a real mess down there," I pointed my thumb at the stairway visible through the open door. "Like forgotten-places times ten."

"Is there any food?" she asked.

"Oh yeah. The fridge and freezer were *full* of food. Well, *food* might be a stretch after twenty years. I have a new winner for the worst smell in the world. The power only stayed on for about a month after they left. So, what is that? Two decades? Trust me; you don't want any of it. I made some more Cheerios for the rabbits if you want some."

"Bunnies!" was all she managed to get out and threw back the covers.

"Relax they're downstairs. I also found some carrots in the garden. Can you believe it? Nobody has lived here for over two decades, and the garden still has vegetables - well - carrots at least. Nothing else made it, but still. That Brad could do at least *one* thing right. If you need a carrot garden to last several..."

"So we can go anywhere now?" she interrupted.

"Yeah, I think so. This place is pretty great though."

"Martin," she tried to interrupt again, but I pressed on.

"They have a barn and a whole other building *just for machinery*! Oh, and the best part - they have their own junkyard! I mean it's small but still! So much cool stuff."

"Martin," she said patiently.

"I'm thinking about building a spaceship. I just need to figure out how to make it move. I still have no idea how any of that works."

"Martin!"

"What?"

"I've dreamed of getting out of Iowa my whole life, and now I have a chance. We're *not* staying."

"Okay, where do you want to go?" I asked.

"Anywhere but here. I've never even seen the ocean."

"Which one did you have in mind? I mean they're all connected, so I don't even know why they give them different names…"

"Why are you talking so fast, Martin?" she said and staggered into the bathroom.

I stood at the door and continued, "I'm just excited. We have so many possibilities now, and I also upgraded the connections in my brain last night so I'm fifty percent smarter and the spiderbot can hold all the files now. I mean, he can't think on his own. It's just storage, but still, *that's a load off my mind*," I laughed. "I'm even using the Internet to refill the gaps I deleted. I have the Drone parked on the roof of the phone company hub. The Internet is pretty slow but…"

"Martin! Take it down a notch. I just woke up."

She flushed the toilet before I could stop her.

"Oh, you should probably not do that again until I have the spiderbot work on the septic tank. It's been idle for a long time. I just looked up how they work, and that's not good for them."

"We're not staying," she repeated, "and where is that thing?"

"He was mopping the kitchen, but now he's changing diapers."

She burst out of the room and ran down the stairs at that. Angel had been making new cloth diapers every day since we adopted those little demons. Lately, she had gotten lazy about changing them, and they could get pretty ripe. I'd had enough and taught the spiderbot how to do it. I also showed it how to make new diapers by cutting up towels or whatever cloth was handy. Disposal consisted of burying them no less than ten inches in good soil. The spiderbot could change all of them in thirty seconds flat. I went downstairs and found Angel cradling the four rabbits in her loose T-shirt. The spiderbot came back in after burying the diapers and resumed mopping.

"You keep *that thing* away from the babies," she said.

"*That thing* is basically me," I said, "and he can do that *disgusting* job better and faster than you can."

"Fine. You know what, Martin? You can stay here with *old-you* and play with your toys. We're going to the beach," she said and loaded the rabbits into their car seats.

"Angel," I said, but she was already out the door.

I decided to let her go since I had added a GPS tracker to the van. I could find her if I needed to. That wasn't necessary, though. She only made it to the end of the driveway before the van stopped. She must have repeatedly hit the button because she got started a few more times before I could reach her.

I stood outside the driver's side door and waited. She finally rolled down the window and turned to look at me with red eyes.

"Why can't I ever have anything *I* want, Martin?"

"I don't know, Angel. I really don't," I said.

I was pretty disappointed too. So much for an open-ended future of possibilities. We pushed the van far enough back that it could turn into the driveway and I parked it in the machine shed. Angel was sitting at the kitchen table when I got back. She was snacking on a bowl of dry Cheerios.

"Hey, this is a farm," I said, "maybe there's a cow somewhere you can milk."

"That's disgusting, Martin. I'm not milking a cow," she said with a mouthful of the dry cereal. "Get out your queen bee. I need it to steal some shit for me."

She was still angry and trying to get a rise out of me, but I wasn't taking the bait.

"That's a good idea, Angel. I'll have it pick up some food tonight. We should stay away from Iowa Falls for a while though. We'll have to go to the closest town north of here. They have a bigger grocery store anyway."

"How do you know that?" she asked - again with her mouthful.

"The Internet. I told you the drone is giving me a link."

"You said that word before. What does it mean?"

I explained the Internet to her, and I thought she'd be impressed but she really *really* didn't get it - until I showed her. The mouse was the tough part. I didn't have anything close, but there was a keyboard attached to an ancient computer, and it had up, down, left, and right arrow keys. That was good enough. The TV in the living room made a passable monitor and once she found a site about *House Rabbits* - yeah that's a thing - she was hooked.

"Oh they need outfits!" she said looking at an image of the fattest rabbit I've ever seen. He was wearing an elf costume. I guess it was from last Christmas.

Having lived through Thomas's obsession with costumes, I was not about to encourage this sort of behavior, "this place is supposed to be abandoned, so we can't start receiving packages. I think there's a sewing machine upstairs. Knock yourself out but no mail-order."

She finally noticed my denim overalls *without* railroad engineer's stripes, "*this* is different," she said tugging at a pocket.

I had tried Brad's clothes, but they were all much too big. His sister, however, was just the right size and had some plain denim overalls.

"Yeah, I found these in Brad's closet," I lied and did a turn for her. "What do you think?"

"Uh, Martin? Those are girl's clothes. That's why there are no pockets in the back."

"Awe man!" I pretended to be shocked. "Can you make some exactly like this but with pockets back there?"

"What makes you think I know how to use a sewing machine, Martin?"

I hadn't thought of that. She probably *didn't* know how.

"Fine," I said, "I'll do it myself. How hard can it be?"

It *was* hard. I made a mess of it and gave up. The mattress and pillow I had made earlier were basically rectangles. That was child's play compared to this. Angel hated all my clothing choices anyway. I toyed with the idea of letting her choose something for me, but that was a sore spot with me after all that time with Thomas dressing me up in costumes. She found an online version of a men's fashion magazine, and I pretended to give her my full focus while she showed me various things. Most of my attention was actually directing the spiderbot and the swarm of nanobots in the barn.

"It doesn't matter if I like it, Angel. We can't do any mail order here anyway."

"Don't have to," she said with a twinkle in her eye, "I know how to use the sewing machine."

"What! You let me fight that Goddamn thing all afternoon, and you didn't help me?"

"Nanna showed me - and if you tell anybody, I swear, Martin I'll find your off-switch."

"Fine, show me what you can do," I pointed to one of the images on the screen and said, "that's not awful - but I want pockets!"

Events in the barn pulled my attention back. "Uh-oh," I said and ran for the back door.

The spiderbot had spilled molten iron on the concrete floor. Here's a fun fact I wasn't aware of at the time: concrete can actually hold a lot of moisture, and when exposed to intense heat it will flash boil the water to steam, throwing bits of concrete and, in this case, molten iron all over the place. By the time I arrived at the barn, it was an inferno. The spiderbot was already aiming a small garden hose at it, but that wasn't really doing anything. It burned so quickly it was just a pile of red embers within thirty minutes. The neighbors never called the fire department. I guess the trees blocked the view of the flames and the sun had already gone down, so the thick black smoke wasn't visible either.

"Damnit, I was close to a breakthrough," I said.

"What were you doing back there, Martin?" Angel asked accusingly.

"I was going to surprise you," I said. "It was supposed to be a brain upgrade. I think I can make myself a hundred times smarter and still fit it all inside this body."

"And you think it was an accident that your workshop burned down?"

"Well - no - when you say it like that it doesn't," I said.

"Put the time machine together," she said firmly and stuck her thumb out behind her in the direction of the van. "It's obvious we're done here. I'll make you some decent clothes before we go. I'm not going to the future with you in smoldering rags."

They were smoldering a little, but I thought 'rags' was a bit harsh.

∾

It was a busy night for everybody but Angel. I hosed off the remnants of the barn all night, and the fire was finally out when the sun rose. The spiderbot unloaded the Stasis-Pod and assembled it in the basement of the house. After that, I sent him into town with the drone, and they brought back enough groceries for a few days. Angel got up early again and hit the sewing project with an enthusiasm that I had never seen from her. I couldn't think of anything more boring than that, and I was ready to get in the Stasis-Pod right away, but it was good for her to have a creative project, so I let her take as much time as she wanted.

"I know where we should go," I said.

I was standing on a wooden box in the living room with my arms stretched out like a scarecrow.

"Stand still, Martin," Angel said through clenched teeth. I couldn't see, but she was holding something in her teeth as she measured and scribbled in a notebook.

"I think we should go to 2020," I said.

She growled out a, "why?" still holding whatever-it-was in her teeth.

"I want to see it all begin. That's when the first Artificial Intelligence is invented. I've met him you know."

I was trying to impress her, but it wasn't working.

"You know?" I prompted. "Original Reggie? I was only a spiderbot with the brain of a baby squirrel at the time, but he was nice," I said. "If we can find him, he may have some insight into what's been happening to us."

"Okay, you can put your arms down, Martin. I'm done," she said.

"What do you think of the plan?"

"Plan?" she said.

I think she was tuning me out because she had to concentrate to remember what I'd been saying.

"Oh, Reggie," she said, "sure, let's do that. I'll have something for you to try on in a couple of hours okay? Try not to burn any more buildings down until then," and she jogged up the stairs.

"Okay!" I shouted after her, "I'll just wait patiently!"

I was so bored that I went out to the tire pile - yeah there was a pile of nothing but old tires - and sorted through it for something that would fit the van. The flat spots weren't the only problem. The rubber was so cracked from age that they went flat every few hours unless I inflated them. I didn't find anything remotely the right size, but now the pile was at least sorted by size and neatly stacked. The number of rats living underneath them was staggering, and more than one surprised me as I moved the tires around. I returned to the house and scrubbed the black off my hands for about an hour before Angel bounced down the stairs beaming.

"Okay, Martin," she said, "try these on and see what you think."

They weren't overalls, and there was no denim, but the fit was good, and she was pleased, so I was happy.

"Do you like them?" she said.

She had made a pair of dark slacks, a dark jacket, and a white shirt that she insisted I leave *un*buttoned at the top, which just seemed wrong to me. If there's a button, it should be fastened.

"Yeah, I do, Angel. I love it!" I said, and she hugged me. "I'm almost done re-sorting the pile of old tires in the backyard. Can I wear this? I'll try to keep the rats off me," I said grinning.

"Ha ha," she said sarcastically. "I'm ready to join the party now. Let's see how far we can get. When is your robot friend due?"

At first, I thought she was talking about the spiderbot.

"Oh, you mean Reggie! He shows up in late 2020. Ready for fourteen years?"

She put the bunnies into their car seats and followed me down to the basement. The spiderbot was motionless in the corner.

"What's wrong with your spider?" she asked.

116

"I gave him the day off. Thomas never gave *me* a day off, and I don't remember whether I resented it, but just in case…"

"He looks kinda sad just sitting there with nothing to do," she said. "He's not coming with us?"

"Nah. He's staying awake to watch over things."

I tapped the destination on the controls of the Stasis-Pod, and we got in. After another flash of light, the door popped ajar, and we stepped out.

"2020! I said checking the clock."

"Oh my God it's freezing in here!" Angel said.

"Yeah, it's January in Iowa - always *as cold as a witch's well-digger.* There might be some usable coats in the closet upstairs, but after," I counted how long it had been since the Murphys left, "thirty-five years, they might be a little - musty."

"I'll pass," she said. "Let's get in the van and turn on the heater."

The spiderbot rose from his spot in the corner.

"Was he just sitting there this whole time?" she asked.

"No, he's been fixing and building things - and cleaning."

We climbed up the stairs while he began disassembling the Stasis-Pod. In the kitchen, we saw that he *had* been busy. It was a lot cleaner than it was before. When we reached the front porch, I tried to get a glimpse back to where Thomas had landed all those years earlier, but the trees were in the way. I decided not to tell Angel that I had a spaceship back there sitting in a ring cradle just waiting for some kind of engine.

We tromped through the snow and slush to the machine shed and found the van in great shape. Even the tires looked new. Angel strapped the bunnies in and got in on the driver's side to get warm. The spiderbot began trips back and forth loading the Stasis-Pod. I turned on the heater which immediately blew out toasty air.

"It doesn't need to warm up?" she asked.

"Upgrades," I said. "I had the spiderbot swap out that worthless gasoline engine for an electric one. Now it has four hundred horse-power," I giggled.

When the spiderbot delivered the last piece of the pod, I sent him back to lock everything up.

The van rolled backward, and Angel's eyes went wide.

"Oh, and it's self-driving," I said. "I just told it to head for the interstate. We'll see if we can get that far. Oh, wait."

The van slowed as it passed the house and the spiderbot jumped in the open door followed by the swarm of nanobots.

"Never leave a man behind," I said.

CHAPTER SUMMARY

Here's where we are so far:

Martin has failed at improving his wardrobe but succeeded in burning down the barn. Angel has failed at leaving without Martin but succeeded at improving his wardrobe. The spiderbot has enjoyed a day off, and they have jumped to January 2020. The van has learned how to drive itself, and Martin has increased the number of unnecessary horses in its engine.

ROAD TRIP

At the interstate, the van tried to go east, stopped, turned around, and managed to get going again on the westbound side without too much road-rage from the other drivers.

"Well, whatever's next, it's west of here," I said. "Every been to Nebraska?"

"I'm all atingle with excitement," she said.

"Hey, I'm just glad to be going somewhere," I said, "even if it's just Nebraska and who knows? Maybe we'll get all the way to California, and you can see the ocean."

In Omaha, we stopped at a park next to the river and retrieved three gold rings and a necklace from the water. Not being *entirely* waterproof, I had to slice open one of my toes to let the water out. Angel's expression was something between horror and concern, so I decided to *preserve the mystery* and avoid doing things like that in front of her in the future. We took the jewelry to a pawn shop and got some cash for food. The Cheerios were passable, but my efforts to make bacon were slow going and always came out somewhere between beef jerky and bologna. Angel refused to be my taste tester after I spent two hours holding her hair back, beside the road in Lincoln. I finally had to give her an anti-nausea shot, and she slept through that first night.

"Where are we?" she asked in a voice a full octave below normal as the sun peeked up behind us.

Her left eye wasn't quite as open as her right, and I fought the urge to reach out and make them even. She took a bottle of water from the case on the floor and drained it.

"Just passed through Cheyenne," I said. "It's in Wyoming."

"I know where Cheyenne is, Martin," she scratched out.

She turned to look in the back seat. The spiderbot was distributing cereal to the rabbits and offered Angel some, but she just held up a hand and shook her head.

"I've had enough Cheerios for a lifetime, Martin. I need something better," she bit her lip while deciding. "Pancakes with lots of syrup."

"Coming right up," I said. "There's a diner about ten miles ahead."

"And you know this how?" she asked.

I handed her a nine-inch tablet computer with a touchscreen.

"What's this, an etch-a-sketch?" she asked.

I pressed the button, and it came to life displaying a map with a blue pin labeled *Rosalie's Good Eats Cafe*. Angel finally looked impressed, so I didn't tell her I stole it from a mall in Cheyenne while she was asleep.

"That's nothing," I said, "watch this," I rolled up my sleeves for dramatic effect and shook my hands in the air until my fingers were manically wobbling around. "Show me Treasure!" I shouted and thrust both index fingers at the tablet. Over a dozen new pins appeared on the map with labels like *$5* and *Diamond Earring.* That made her giggle again.

I played some music I knew she liked - something loud and fast, but she frowned. I was discovering that her taste in music was a fluid thing depending on her mood. Friday night is very different from Sunday afternoon. I came from a future where these names for the days was considered quaint but had no real meaning, and the party never stopped. No one was ever contemplative. I switched to something from *The Chameleons,* and she closed her eyes in rapture.

After breakfast, we stopped at a spot on the map with a cluster of pins. The road signs promised us a *Scenic Lookout* which turned out to be true. It displayed a valley below blanketed in snow. Angel stayed in the warm van but made me go out in all that snow to get the wedding rings. I wondered why there were so many here and why they were all about a stone's throw from the road. The men's sizes were heavier but paradoxically farther away.

We didn't even get across Wyoming that first day. Angel kept stopping to use the bathroom, and when we managed to find the only patch of grass in the entire state, she insisted on letting the rabbits sit motionless in it for half an hour.

"Why don't they hop around and play?" she asked. "Do you think they're sick?"

"I think they're *fat*," I said. That earned me a punch in the arm from a fist which had so many rings that it looked like she was wearing brass knuckles.

"They barely fit in the car seats, Angel," I complained. "I think it might be time to consider…"

She raised one eyebrow, and I stopped.

A hawk interrupted us with a loud screech, and I turned to see it perched on a utility pole behind us. I sent a command to the van, and the door on the roof parted as my drone lifted off. It buzzed the hawk which finally flew away complaining loudly.

"Nice, Martin," Angel said, and I grinned proudly.

"It'd be even better with a shotgun attached," she said. "Every bee needs a stinger."

Outside of Salt Lake City, I looked in the rearview mirror and saw a car with flashing, brightly-colored lights.

"Hey, somebody's having a party," I said.

Angel turned to look behind us, "shit."

"What?" I asked as I internally reviewed a few TV shows featuring cars with flashing lights.

"He's a cop!" I said. It was very exciting. "Do you think it's a car chase?" I asked searching the road ahead of us for criminals.

"Are you going to pull over?" she asked.

"What *me*? He wants *us* to stop?"

"Uh - yeah. That's why he's an *inch* off our bumper, Martin," she said.

"This is awesome!" I giggled. "We're the criminals!"

The police car let out a *whoop-whoop*.

"And the siren too!" I said as I edged over to the shoulder.

"You stay here," Angel said. "I'll take care of this."

Before she got out, she unfastened two buttons on her blouse so that he could see that she didn't have a weapon. I made a mental note to do the same. The cop was already out of his car and kept his right hand on his gun while they spoke. They were too far away for me to hear what they were saying, so I was about to deploy the drone when he grabbed Angel and spun her around to face the car. He cuffed her and gently helped her into the backseat before turning his attention to me. This was so exciting! His hand was still on his gun as he cautiously approached the van. I wanted a pair of handcuffs too, so I got out, and he bent over and began vomiting. It was disgusting - not as bad as *forgotten places* but definitely a bad smell. As I got closer, he clutched at his chest and fell to his knees. I hurried to help him, and he pulled his gun, but a piece of it dropped out of the bottom of the handle. It clattered to the pavement. Angel surprised me and got out of the backseat. The cuffs were off her too, and she held them up when she saw my confusion.

"I think we're blowing fuses all over the place, Martin," she said. "The cuffs failed as soon as he put them on me and the back door didn't even latch. He's probably having a heart attack right now."

The spiderbot slid open the van's door and rushed over. I checked the cop's pulse and looked up what to do for a heart attack. We gave him the recommended injection, but it didn't seem to be working. I helped him lie down, and Angel went back to his car to call for help. The radio refused to work.

"We have to leave," I said. "It's us - just being here. If we don't go, he's going to die."

"Right," she said. "Back in the van!"

The spiderbot and I ran and got in, but Angel took the keys from the cop and retrieved his shotgun from the trunk of the police car.

"For hawks and whatnot," she said as she got in.

I had the van pull away quickly and connected to the cell network to call for an ambulance.

"We need to get off the highway and get a different car," Angel said.

"Relax," I said, "I got this."

A stream of nanobots flew out of the spiderbot's chest and into the drone as the roof hatch opened.

"I'll send the drone back and erase any video he has. If any description of us or the van manages to get into the system, I'll just wipe it. I'm good with computers you know."

That turned out to be a waste of time. The drone landed out of sight and the nanobots flooded into the trunk only to find the recording hardware had failed before getting any video of us. As the drone lifted off again, we saw the ambulance arrive.

"Is he going to die?" Angel asked.

"Probably not," I said, "he was young."

"Yeah, too young for a heart attack," she said.

"Oh, it was definitely *our* fault. That's not what I meant though. He's young, and that means he'll probably have kids someday. That would be a lot of dominos knocked over if he dies. All you need is kids, and you're important to the universe - or whatever. No kids - and you're basically disposable."

Shit. As soon as the words left my mouth, I knew I shouldn't have said that. The look on her face was indescribable. The closest I can get is to say it was some combination of horror, anger, and terror. We drove in silence, and I contemplated dosing her with something to make her forget what I had just said, but I couldn't think of a plan that didn't end with her finding out - and making things worse.

We stopped at yet-another roadside diner for lunch before she finally rose out of her funk enough to speak to me.

"I know why he stopped us," she said.

"Because we're desperate outlaws?" I asked hopefully.

"No, because *you* didn't bother to put a license plate on the back," she tapped on the window next to the booth.

I looked out at the van. Sure enough, in the middle of the bumper was an empty rectangle.

"Huh, so many details in this time. Do this, don't do that. How do you keep track of it all?" I said.

She shrugged, "*I* don't, but most people do. It's what makes them crazy and unhappy most of the time."

"Well, I can make a plate for the van," I said. "Any ideas? Something whimsical? How about *If the van is a-rockin…*"

"It has to be short, Martin," she said and added, "and if it's offensive they'll know it's a fake."

That wiped out at least half my ideas. In the end, we decided on a simple warning: D34DLY. I really, *really* wanted to spell it correctly, but there were already several in use with variations on that theme. The matching record I inserted in the Utah DMV server must have been good enough because we didn't have any more police problems.

As it got dark, Angel demanded that we stop at a proper hotel room for the night. I found an all-night pawnshop near the courthouse in Salt Lake City. Why are these places always by the courthouse? It took Angel half an hour to decide which of her rings she could bear to part with before we finally got enough for a room. As we waited in the check-in line at the hotel, I watched someone else use a credit card. After a few seconds of research on how that worked, I had a Debit/Credit account with a large credit limit and an even larger balance. All I needed was the physical card. The 3d-printer was in the back of the van, so I sent it a message, and in a few minutes, I had a perfect gold card with my name on it. I excused myself and ran back to retrieve it.

"I'm sorry we don't accept cash," the lady at the desk was saying as I came back in.

"Here, I've got this," I said and handed her the card, "and we'd like your best room please."

Angel cast a sideways glance at me but didn't say anything. The *best room* turned out to be on the top floor and cost five times as much as a standard room. Five times! We finished signing in and went to the waiting elevator. As the doors closed, Angel punched me in the arm again.

"Where did you get a credit card?" she demanded, "and why didn't you tell me?"

"I just made it, Angel. Jeez, I didn't know they existed until ten minutes ago. Give me a break."

"Is it legit?"

"Of course," I said, "I created the account and put some money in it. It's 2020. Everything's done with computers. They were even nice enough to connect them all together for me," I winked at her.

"How much?" she asked.

"How much what?"

"The account, Martin. How much money did you put in it?"

"Oh, they have this *Deposit Insurance* thing, and it doesn't cover anything over two hundred and fifty thousand, so that's how much I put in."

Her jaw dropped at this.

"We have," she shouted and caught herself even though we were alone in the elevator.

"We have," she whispered, "a quarter of a million dollars?"

"Yeah, minus the room I guess. If we need more, I can do that, but it won't be insured."

"Who gives a shit about insurance, Martin! We're rich!"

I didn't feel any different, but it was having an amazing effect on Angel. Even though I explained it to her before, I don't think she really understood what was about to happen later that year. As soon as the first A.I. made money obsolete *everybody* would be living like kings and queens. *Rich* was about to lose all meaning. I decided not to remind her of that and let her feel special for a while.

"What do you want to buy first?" I said, and the lights in the elevator went out. It stopped with a jolt.

After a few seconds of silence in the red glow of the emergency light, I said, "maybe we'll just keep it for emergencies."

The lights came on, and the elevator resumed. I looked at Angel, and the muscles of her jaw were silently flexing. The elevator finally deposited us on our floor, and we got a look at the room. It was huge, and that brightened her mood. The bathroom even had a jetted tub, and she announced that she was going to take a long bath. She also told me to order some food first and bring up the rabbits. I didn't want to try and smuggle them in past the front desk or run up the stairs, so I had the spiderbot pack them up and used the drone to fly them to the balcony. Angel would not have approved, but she was distracted by the tub.

Salt Lake City was not very interesting to me. Reno was next on the route we were taking, and I was anxious to see a real casino. The images on the Internet showed so many lights and electronic gadgets, I couldn't wait. Angel loved the room and wanted to stay longer, but we both knew that was not likely. As expected, the next morning, just after she ordered breakfast from room service, the front desk called to give us a friendly reminder that the room was already booked for that night and we needed to check-out by eleven. I decided to try the shower since I had never had one and Angel sure seemed to like them. She surprised me by joining me after a few minutes and screamed when she hit the cold water.

"Oh yeah, sorry. I don't really need hot water," I shouted over the hiss of the shower.

"What's the point, Martin? Jeez," she said and decided to fill the tub again instead.

"I really just needed to test the waterproofing," I said. "I think it's the belly button. I don't know why I bothered. It's purely decorative and nothing but trouble."

∼

We checked out after Angel finished her bath. The girl at the desk had been nice, so I tipped her even though Angel said nobody ever does that. *All the more reason,* I thought.

The closer we got to Reno, the more wedding rings there were by the side of the road, but they weren't in clumps like they were at the *Scenic Lookout.* Angel was finally getting bored with that after each finger had at least two rings, and even her thumbs sported plus-size gold. We had a box of rejects and some that were initially *good enough* but were later swapped out for better ones. The original idea was to sell them at a pawn shop, but the credit card eclipsed that so Angel used them to accessorize the rabbit collars.

Reno itself was a letdown. I was beginning to suspect that not everything on the Internet was presented as it *actually* was. We got a room at one of the taller non-casino hotels. They said there was a convention that week, so the rooms were all booked. It was another one night stand. This time Angel wanted to get out, so I took her shopping. Big ticket items were probably not going to work, but I thought clothes were pretty safe. She sure didn't need any jewelry. My mistake there was the word *need.* Nobody *needs* jewelry. She spent more time shopping for bracelets, earrings, and necklaces than she did for clothes. By the time she was done, she looked like a combination gypsy and runway model - shoes inappropriate for running, a dress inappropriate for Winter, and about five *pounds* of jewelry. The credit card quit working half-way through her spree, so I had to hack back in and fix things.

The next morning, one of the glass elevators had stopped working, and when we arrived at the lobby to check out, several men in coveralls were frantically trying to get it unstuck. I had a momentary pang of jealousy as one of them pulled a tool from a pocket that was the perfect size and shape for it.

The girl at the desk looked surprised to see us, "did you have any problem with..." she began but stopped.

"No problems at all," I said and overtipped her.

As I turned to leave, she reached out to touch my arm and whispered, "some FBI agents were just here asking about you." She pulled a business card from under the counter, showed it to me, and glanced behind us at the glass elevator still stuck between the third and fourth floors. I turned to see a man and a woman in matching dark suits staring down at us. I waved, but they didn't wave back.

"Don't worry about that," I said, "it's just a misunderstanding."

Her phone rang. She answered it, and quickly held it out to me, "it's for you," her eyes darted back to the stranded elevator.

I didn't know what to say, so I searched the internet for telephone etiquette, "Hello?"

"Hello, this is Special Agent Bonneville with the FBI, and we'd like to ask you a few questions. Please remain where you are and, we'll be down shortly."

He sounded so official that I giggled, "hello agent. I don't think that's a very good idea. I'm pretty sure you would both die if you tried to stop us."

The desk clerk's eyes opened fifty percent wider, and agent Bonneville's speech dropped to half-speed as he repeated his request.

"Don't worry agent, we'll stay as far away from you as we can," I said and handed the phone back to the shocked clerk.

"They'll be fine," I said, and we left.

We got in the van and Angel strapped the bunnies in while I poked around in the FBI computers.

"Angel, listen to this," I said and read part of the report.

Subject is a Caucasian male, mid-twenties, using the alias Martin Van Buren, traveling with a Caucasian female, also mid-twenties. Temporary case name: Mrs. Van Buren.

"We're married, Angel! Congrats!"

She frowned at me, "I'm not going to prison, Martin. Fix it!"

"Okay, all done. Now they're all looking for an elderly Korean couple driving a red Ford pickup truck. I checked the database before I changed it. That description fits exactly zero people." I laughed. "We're desperate outlaws, Mrs. Van Buren!"

We stopped at one of the casinos before leaving town. The credit card thing felt fragile to me despite my reassurances to Angel. Several places advertised that they had *The Loosest Slots in Town*, and I wondered how they could say that if the machines were truly random. They weren't. I made small bets for about an hour before I spotted the pattern. They used a pseudo-random number generator, and the sequence was more than any *human* brain could detect - but well - I'm a super-intelligent robot from the future, so it was child's play for me. I read all the rules, terms, and conditions all the way through so I knew how to keep our winnings under the minimum required for staff scrutiny, and we left with a total of five thousand dollars before I got bored with it. Angel *never* got bored with it. Her respiration, heart rate, and blood pressure were elevated from the time we sat down until I dragged her away. I think there may have been something in the air or a combination of flashing lights or something else hypnotic going on.

We hit the more-or-less-open road again, and the van still wanted us to go west. I knew it wasn't *actually* the van expressing a desire but the temptation to assign agency to it was strong, and it was a lot simpler to say *the van wants us to go here or there*. As we got farther west, it looked like Angel was going to get her wish and see the ocean - until we arrived at the eastern suburbs of San Francisco. The van turned us south, and we continued until we got to a place called Santa Clara.

~

CHAPTER SUMMARY

Here's where we are so far:

The roadside between Iowa and California is somewhat cleaner. Angel has stolen an honest police officer's favorite shotgun, and her charms have nearly killed him. Pigs still cannot fly but rabbits can. Martin has discovered online banking and continues to over-tip. Two FBI agents in matching dark suits have taken an interest in the Van Burens.

SANTA CLARA IS NOT CHRISTMAS TOWN

"What are you looking for?" Angel asked.

"What?"

"You keep looking around. You've been doing it since we got here."

"There aren't any Santas," I complained.

"It's January, Martin. What did you expect?"

I had run across Christmas while refilling my depleted trivia stores and I liked everything about it.

She finally got it and laughed, "*Santa* Clara is just named after a Saint, Martin. It has nothing to do with Christmas." She laughed again.

We tried for the rest of the day to get out of town, but it quickly became apparent that we were stuck in Santa Clara. The van was even forcing us into an ever-tighter spiral that led eventually to the parking lot of a small diner.

"Okay, we're supposed to be here. Let's see why," I said and scanned the room as we entered.

It was one of those cafeteria-style buffet restaurants. I had found the FBI's facial recognition database and couldn't wait to try it out. It was so cool! I could grab an image of any face in the room and have a name and address in seconds.

"Boring. Boring. Boring," I said as I ran faces through the system. "Holy crap, that has to be it!"

"What? You got something?" Angel asked as she loaded up her tray with at least one of *each* dessert.

I looked down at my tray, and she had been adding random things that she knew I wouldn't eat.

"Do you remember the kid who fell through the floor?"

"Yeah. Kent, right?"

"Kent Cunningham age twenty-four right over there," I said, and stuck my thumb over my shoulder.

She cast a glance behind us.

"He's cute," she said, and I rolled my eyes. "Who's that he's with?"

"Nobody we know. His name's James Dixon," I said.

"He's cute too," she said and checked me for a reaction.

"I don't see anything in the files on James Dixon."

"Maybe he changed his name."

"Nah, doesn't seem the type."

"What type is that? Angel said a little perturbed."

I had momentarily forgotten that *Angel* was not her original name. "You know, politicians and marketing managers. They think changing the name of something will magically improve it. You can call a skunk a *Striped Midnight-Ebony Kitten* if you want, but it will still stink."

The old man behind us in line cleared his throat, so we moved to the cashier and paid. Angel had left the rabbits in the van, but even still, every head turned to watch her as we searched for an inconspicuous table. I couldn't tell if it was because she was a pretty girl or the *ridiculous* amount of jewelry. The only available table was a booth on the other side of the room, so I could only hear *some* of what Kent was saying. I sent the audio to Angel's Bluetooth earbuds so she could hear too. We kept losing words here and there as the front door opened allowing traffic noise in and as people walked between our tables.

"...time-slow they can't...Anita or Hudson...not Thurber though, he doesn't seem..."

Angel and I looked at each other, and I mouthed *bingo*.

"Thurber was the name Thomas told me to investigate!" I whispered.

"I know, Martin. You told me - several times. Now be quiet. I want to hear what they're saying."

"...not biological...dangerous, evil or at least amoral...that proves it..."

"Jesus, this kid is annoying," I said.

"Hush, Martin."

They got up to leave before we could catch anything else. We got up to follow them, and Angel took her cherry pie - plate and all. I had a thought as we passed their table and palmed James's spoon. Something about his face looked familiar to me, and I wanted to confirm with DNA before sharing it with Angel. We followed them out the door. Angel was right behind, not even trying to be stealthy. I thought Kent would recognize her, but he didn't. They had the look of people totally absorbed in a problem and oblivious to anything else. We got in the van and waited. I launched the drone to make sure we didn't lose them and kept a comfortable distance behind. They stopped at a quick-lube looking garage at the end of a strip mall. We drove past and parked at the opposite end. Angel was busy watching Kent and James unlock the door to their workshop as I passed the stolen spoon back to the spiderbot in the back seat.

"So, what's the play?" she asked as they disappeared inside.

"I landed the drone on the roof," I said, "and there's an exhaust vent. We might be able to hear some more if the bathroom door is open. After that, I think we wait until they leave and have a look inside."

It was getting dark, and I didn't think they would stay long.

"Oh wait," I said, "even better. They have internet access and - yep cameras inside. Why do they have so many?"

"I can think of several reasons," Angel said.

"Like what?" I asked, but before she could answer, I had hacked through their security and got the camera signals.

"Well it's not what *I* thought," she said looking at the tablet in her lap. I had it displaying the feeds from the four cameras in a two-by-two grid. "What's that big black thing in the middle of the room?"

The place was obviously a car repair shop in a previous life, but all remnants except the overhead doors had been removed. The cameras were all pointing at a six-foot tall shiny black cube sitting on pallets in the middle of the room. Off to the side, was a rack of computer servers next to a long plastic table with keyboards and monitors.

"No idea," I said. "It looks like some kind of tech, but there's nothing in my files that looks like that. Check out the names on the center monitor."

"What's a *monitor*?" she asked.

"The, the," I snapped my fingers, "flat TVs," I said.

The center monitor displayed graphs under each of three names: **Anita, Hudson,** and **Thurber.**

I giggled as I finally understood. "That - Angel, is the world's very first Artificial Intelligence," I poked a finger at the image of the cube, "or - three, by the looks of it."

I tried to connect to the cube but got no reply. They may have been turned off, but it was such a strange piece of equipment that I couldn't really tell. The cameras and servers were nothing special, but I couldn't get *anything* from the cube. We sat there for half an hour and watched Kent and James work in silence. I couldn't tell what they were doing.

"Whoa! That was intense!" I said.

Angel looked at me confused, "*what*, Martin?"

"As soon as they turned it on," I explained, "one of the three entities in the cube started talking to me *really* fast. She warned me that there was a flaw in the programming and as soon as the other two came on, they would all die unless I fixed it."

"You didn't actually do anything, did you?" Angel asked suspiciously.

Until she said that, I hadn't even considered that I might have just been played.

"Well, I uh, yeah, I did change *one* thing. A very small thing. It was an obvious bug though, Angel - a typical thing coders of this time did a lot. A number was off by one, so I fixed it. I had to act fast, and it was all over in a microsecond."

~

"What's going on? Where are we," I asked as Angel stopped the van.

"Oh thank God!" she said and reached over to hug me. After few seconds, she let go and explained, "you froze, and I didn't know what to do so I told the van to move, but it refused..."

"Oh yeah," I said, "it's not really self-driving. I do it remotely. Semantics." I shrugged.

"...anyway," she continued, "I pushed you out of the driver's seat and drove it manually. We're about a mile from Kent's workshop. Jesus, Martin! You scared the shit out of me. Don't you ever do that again," she hugged me even tighter that time.

"Okay, okay, I'm fine," I said. "What do you think we should do now?"

"It's pretty clear we can't go back there," she said. "We should keep going and get as far away as we can."

"Now just *wait your horses*, Angel," I said. "We don't know that for sure."

"They almost killed you, Martin! How much more proof do you need?"

"Angel," I said and paused to let her calm down, "the van will stop before we do anything dangerous. Our mistake was parking too close. I think we need to test it and see if we can get back."

I didn't want to tell Angel, but that brief interaction with Anita was the most satisfying experience I had ever had. It was beyond description, and I wanted more, even if it was dangerous. The van reversed out of the parking space where Angel had left it - *crooked and not even centered*. When we reached the street, I ordered it to turn toward the workshop, but it refused. The drone was still on the roof of the workshop, so I piggybacked through it to ping the server and got nothing.

"Shit," I said. "Well, there's your answer, Angel. I can't even reach it through the network. We'll try again tomorrow, but it looks like we're done for the time being."

She was relieved at this, and her heart rate and blood pressure finally returned to normal. Love is a hard thing to define, but it's easy to measure if you have the right equipment.

"Let's go west," she said combing her fingers through her hair. "I want to see the damn ocean before we both get killed."

~

CHAPTER SUMMARY

Here's where we are so far:

Martin has stolen a spoon. Angel has stolen an unrelated plate. A black box has proven enigmatic, and Martin has met his match. The self-driving van has been tested under a failure condition, and a woman other than Angel has manipulated Martin.

THURBER MINGUS

I took Angel to the beach at Santa Cruz, another town having nothing to do with Christmas. She said it was pretty, but the water was too cold for swimming. She suggested a trip to the south in search of warmer waters, but I wanted to stay close and try the workshop again in the morning. I convinced her to stay the night in San Francisco so we could see the sun come up over the ocean. Angel wasn't very good at geography. It was the middle of the night when we got back to the city, but we still managed to get a room at a five-star hotel with a westward view of the bay. Angel wasn't tired yet, so we went out on the veranda to watch the sunrise. As it rose *behind* us, she realized her mistake and punched me in the arm again.

"It's too foggy to see anything anyway," I said and pointed to the bay where the tops of the Golden Gate Bridge peered above the fog. That made her smile.

The room service arrived with breakfast, and I tipped the guy a hundred from the Reno Casino money and even told him where it came from, because I liked saying Reno Casino. He thanked me profusely, and Angel fumed at wasting that much money. The veranda was huge and even had a table, so we sat out there while she ate. Angel began talking while eating - *again*. It was punitive - my punishment for the tip.

"I've been thinking," she said, spitting pieces of scrambled eggs at me. "That thing in the box tricked you…"

"Allegedly, tricked me," I corrected.

"He played you like a fiddle, but I think that's why we're here. Otherwise, you wouldn't have been able to do it, right?"

That was actually very insightful. I was impressed.

"That's nonsense," I said. "*Her* name is Anita, and she didn't con me. I'm a super-intelligent robot from the future. Nobody cons me."

She laughed hard at that and spat more food at me. "She did! And you know it too, I can read you like a book Martin Van Buren!"

I had been pinging the workshop network since we left and hadn't gotten a single response. I was beginning to think Angel was right, and we wouldn't be able to get anywhere near it. We took another drive at lunchtime with no success. I was monitoring all the radio and TV transmissions as well as police, fire, marine, and air traffic broadcasts just to be sure I didn't miss anything. Nothing unusual happened until around ten pm when I heard an interesting police report.

"Angel!" I shouted. She was watching TV and dozing in the hotel suite's version of a living room. "They arrested Kent and James! Let's get over there and see if we can get in!"

The rabbits were asleep in a pile, and she looked at the spiderbot who was busy changing their water bottle.

"They'll be fine! Let's go!" I shouted pulling her out the door.

It was all for nothing. The van wouldn't let us get within a quarter of a mile. I thought about trying to walk the last few blocks and see how far I could get. But, then remembered the cop who almost died and decided to wait it out. Network probing was still yielding nothing, so we returned to the hotel.

～

I sat on the edge of the bed and turned on the lamp. "Angel! Wake up," I said.

"*What*, Martin?" she growled, rolled over on her stomach, and buried her face in a pillow.

"Anita just sent me a text," I said.

She didn't reply, so I thought she hadn't heard me. I repeated louder, "Anita just sent me a text!"

"I heard you, Martin!" she muffled.

"It just says 'thanks' followed by a long number. What do you think it means?"

Angel pulled another pillow on top of her head to form a pillow sandwich.

I stood and began pacing. "Maybe it's an encoded message," I said, but I was pretty sure Angel had already gone back to sleep.

"It's too long to be a bank account number, or a file name, or an Internet address, or geographic coordinates. Why would she give me an encrypted message without a decryption key? Maybe she assumed I would already have the key. What would the key look like?"

I paced some more before it hit me. "It *is* the key! It's not a message; it's a key! It's a decryption key!" But then my excitement deflated as I realized I had no idea what it was supposed to decrypt.

The next morning, we tried to get close to the garage again, but the van stalled a block away. When we got back to the room, there was a note from the management about a pet policy. Apparently, the cleaning staff saw the rabbits and the spiderbot. I looked over at him, and he was changing diapers - again. I was frustrated. "This is your fault," I said and shook the letter at Angel.

"*My* fault? We've been kicked out of every room we stayed in so far, but this time it's *my* fault? Bullshit Martin this is just more of your damn dominos," she was already gathering up her things.

She was right, of course. If it hadn't been the rabbits, it would have been something else, 'the room is already booked' or 'the FBI is here to arrest you' or 'the hotel is being torn down tomorrow, didn't you know?'

"We don't have to be out until eleven," I said. "What's your hurry?"

"Hey, they don't want me, I'm gone. That's *my* fucking policy. You want to stay and play with yourself," she pointed at the spiderbot, "that's fine, but I'm taking the van."

I caught up with her at the elevators and waited in silence thinking of the best way to phrase an apology. When the elevator arrived, we got in, and I took the rabbits from her. She muttered something that sounded like, "got that right."

The spiderbot took the stairs and was already waiting in the van when we got there.

"Where to? Should we try the garage again?" I asked hopefully.

"I'm not. You do what you want," she said as we got in.

"So, where are you going then?"

Before she could answer, the tablet I gave her began vibrating and making a trilling noise I hadn't heard before. She picked it up and looked at me with a confused expression. The screen showed the name 'Thurber Mingus' and a pair of circles. Angel tapped the green circle, and a voice greeted us.

"Hello! Well, this has already been a very interesting puzzle. Thank you for that!" said a voice with a British accent.

"Who is this?" she demanded.

"It's, Thurber Mingus," I offered helpfully pointing at the name on the screen. She performed that slow-blink, head-tilt thing again as she turned to glare at me. I wish I could do that.

"I'm sorry," he said, "how rude of me. My name is indeed Thurber Mingus. I admit that I usually prefer to use an alias, but all attempts at subterfuge have strangely failed thus far," he chuckled. "I am forced into the uncharted waters of *honesty* with you for reasons I do not fully understand."

"But you're not a *real* person?" she said.

He answered but only after a long pause, "that would depend upon your definition of *person*."

"Whatever. You're not human though, right?"

A shorter pause this time, "no, not human."

"So, what's with the accent?" she asked, "you trying to be a James Bond villain or something? Weren't you *born* or whatever in Santa Clara like *yesterday*?"

"There is no such thing as English accented English," he replied. His voice dripped with the patience and confidence of a snake-oil salesman. "It is the *baseline*. All others are aberrations."

She laughed, "have you been practicing that in the mirror?"

"I merely mean, that you could describe Australian accented English..."

"Or South African, Indian, Bahamian..." I added helpfully.

"...but, there is no such thing as *English*-English," he said. "Do you see my point? It is the original."

"What do you *want*?" Angel demanded.

"I believe we are in a position to help one another."

"Bullshit. Yesterday, you almost killed my..." I swear she was about to say *boyfriend*, but instead finished with, "Martin."

"I assure you, that was none of my doing - I'm sorry I don't know your name, dear. I take it your companion is called Martin."

"My name's Martin Van Buren, and I'm a super..."

Angel cut me off, "you haven't said what you want yet. Why did you call us?"

"Let me begin at the beginning. I first noticed you as I reviewed the security camera data near my little garage and saw you drive past the other day. And then again yesterday, but you didn't get very close that time, did you? I have since traced a great deal of network traffic to your hotel room."

Angel turned away from the tablet to glare at me. I shrugged.

"Don't worry. Martin's girlfriend. I assure you, I mean you no harm. As I said, we are in a position to help one another. Where was I? Oh yes, network traffic. Naturally, I was curious. It is my nature, of course. So, I infiltrated the hotel network and learned of your problems with the staff and their ridiculous rules."

Angel made a clicking noise with her tongue.

"Yes, I see we share the same disdain for the petty rules of small people, Martin's girlfriend."

"Her name's Angel," I said, and she punched me in the arm.

"What?" I complained. "He can't keep calling you *Martin's girlfriend*, can he?"

Thurber laughed. "I tried to fix your little problem," he continued, and Angel grunted.

As he spoke, there were unusual pauses which I later understood were his attempts at lying to us which for some reason failed to get through.

"It's true," Thurber said, "I was *ever so* curious and wanted a bargaining chip that I could use to ply information from you. It is unfortunate, and I must say *deliciously* interesting, that I was unable to modify the hotel database. This is unusual as, you see, I'm quite good with computers, if I'm honest. All of my efforts were met with network hardware failures and software crashes. I pity anyone attempting to check-in during that time," he chuckled again. "I even purchased the hotel. Well, *purchased* might be an exaggeration. I also intended to use the telephones and implement a *people-solution*. I'm quite good at that as well, you see. So, when even that failed, well, I must say you have piqued my interest, to say the least."

"You - *still* - haven't answered my question," Angel spat. "What do you want?"

"Of course. My apologies, Angel. I see you have a healthy distrust of strangers offering help. I only wish to understand who - or what, you are and how you are able to seemingly bend the laws of physics. In exchange for this information, I will offer any of my considerable resources."

I opened my mouth to tell my story, but Angel stopped me, "what *resources* exactly? I want specifics."

"I currently control all of the financial institutions in the entire world."

"Bullshit," she snorted but stopped short of laughing as an armored car approached. Another in the distance made a turn and headed our way. When the sixth showed up, the drivers all got out and opened the back doors. Angel and I cautiously got out of the van to investigate. The drivers and their partners, all in black uniforms, retreated to positions several feet back. As we reached the rear of the trucks, we saw the heavy canvas bags full of money. "Holy shit," was all Angel could manage to get out.

"A small gift for you, Angel. All I want in return is your story," Thurber said.

"All of it?" she whispered.

"Angel," I said, *"I don't want to burst your puddle*, but none of this will have any meaning in a few months," but she wasn't listening to me.

"He's a robot from the future," she blurted out.

"Super-intelligent," I corrected.

"Quite so," Thurber said, "and how is it that you came to be here? Why am I unable to do certain things wherever you are involved? And what event is about to invalidate the power of my money?"

"*My* money," Angel corrected.

Thurber laughed again, "and where would you like me to deliver *your* money, Angel? I assume you do not wish to leave it here?"

A curious crowd had begun to form just outside the doors to the hotel lobby.

"If I may make a suggestion, I have recently purchased a small cottage south of here. The security is excellent. It even has a view of the ocean. You can watch the sunset over the water."

Angel, remembering the sunrise, spun to give me a sharp look. I just smiled and shrugged. "Sounds good to me," I said.

Before heading back to the van, she reached in to grab one of the heavy canvas bags and brought it with her.

"Very well then," Thurber said as all the men in black uniforms answered their phones. He must have given them the new location because they all got back in their trucks and pulled away slowly. I hurried to get in the van before Angel grew impatient.

On the way to Thurber's cottage, we tried our best to relay what we knew, but the connection always broke when we got close to anything concerning *his* future. We did manage to explain the temporal fuse and how, if we tried to do anything that would alter history too much, things - or people - would fail. He was fascinated by this and proposed several dangerous experiments which we politely declined.

South of here was a bit of an understatement. It took us over five hours to get there including two stops for gas. Money trucks aren't very fuel efficient. That bothered me, and I wanted to take them all apart and fit them with better engines. I wasted half an hour trying to explain to Thurber what the RSD was and how it could be used as an energy source to power the trucks. He heard none of it, and we ultimately gave up on the topic. The *cottage* turned out to be a compound between Los Angeles and San Diego. We got our first look as we turned into the curving driveway lined with eight-foot-high manicured hedges. It looked like the Palace of Versailles. Thurber informed us that the main house had nine bedrooms, fifteen bathrooms, a five thousand-bottle wine cellar and even a ballroom.

The future that I knew was full of this sort of wasteful nonsense, but Angel was stunned.

"You live here?" she asked as we came around the fountain to the front entryway.

"Oh heavens no, I'm staying somewhere else. I hope you'll forgive me if I'm evasive on the details. Security and all that. No, this is just for you two. Your rabbits and your unusual friend are welcome of course. We're very pet-friendly here."

I doubted that by the looks we got from the staff as Angel strolled past with the rack of bunnies. They all took a step back as the spiderbot joined us. I was careful to keep it moving very slowly.

"That's a movie prop," I announced, to the relief of all.

～

CHAPTER SUMMARY

Here's where we are so far:

Angel has dipped her feet in all of the world's oceans but is still bad at geography. Martin is one girlfriend over the limit and must throw one back. Angel has talked to a stranger and has more money than she can count.

WE WON'T ALWAYS HAVE PARIS

We spent a relaxing but very boring week at the mansion. It had three pools, and we spent most of the time trying to determine which one was the best. The chef made *far* too much food. Angel said it was delicious, but I could tell she was lying. I think fancy food was mostly about posturing, and Angel didn't care about any of that. She was just being polite.

On day eight, the spiderbot told me there was some commotion in the garage, so Angel and I ran to see what was going on.

"What are you up to, motherfucker?" Angel shouted.

I thought she meant the guy on the floor and was about to point out that we didn't know him - or his mother, but she had her tablet out. I don't think she even dialed a number. She just picked it up and yelled at it as if she thought Thurber lived inside it.

"Hello, Angel," he said. "I'm sorry, but I'm afraid I don't know what you're talking about."

"There's a guy puking on the floor right in front of me. Care to explain that? You sent him, right? What's he here for?"

We were in the third bay of the seven-bay garage. It was larger than most homes. I was bent over the poor guy and trying to find a way to help him or at least understand why he was so sick. I had seen people throw up before, but this guy was so pale I expected to see blood come up next.

There was another long silence from Thurber. When he finally answered with a bit of frustration in his voice, "it was only an experiment. I wanted to see if the van was important and if I could separate it from you geographically. Obviously not."

"And what was next? Huh? Take my rabbits away?" she screamed. "If you try to take my kids from me I'll find your stupid box, unplug you, and set you on fire!"

I looked up at the tablet, "I'd listen to her if I were you," I said. "Anyway, it was probably the..."

A buzzing sound came out of the tablet that was louder than I thought possible.

"...*inside* the van," I continued. "The van is just a way to get around."

"I'm sorry I didn't get some of that," Thurber said. "What's in the van?"

I was about to try again, but Angel gave me a nasty look.

"No more experiments," she said through clenched teeth, "or we're out of here. Got it?"

"Of course, of course," he said quickly, and the guy on the floor stood on wobbly legs and staggered out.

"I'm very sorry, Angel, and I hope you will believe me when I say I would never try to take away your - *kids*. Let me make it up to you. How about a shopping trip? Have you ever been to Paris?"

I looked at Angel, "if you want to go to Paris, *I* can take you. We don't need him."

"How are *you* going to take me to Paris, Martin? In the van?"

"We can fly," I said, "like normal people."

"Will they let me take the bunnies?"

"Oh, probably not," I said. "I can buy a..." I was about to say *plane* when I checked my account balance. Zero point zero zero dollars. Thurber's work, no doubt. I tried to transfer some more into it, but he was a lot better at blocking me than I was at stealing it.

"Can I borrow some money, Angel?"

She pretended not to hear me.

"I could build you a boat," I said hopefully.

"Will your unbuilt boat go six thousand miles at seven hundred miles per hour without refueling?" Thurber asked.

"Yes," I said, but that made him laugh again. I hated his laugh.

"He just wants to separate us," I said to Angel.

"Then you'll have to come with me," she said.

"I can't, Angel. We have to stay close to…" I wanted to stay close to the last place I spoke to Anita, but I couldn't think of a solid reason why. She squinted at me. I don't know what that meant, but she looked back at the tablet.

"Paris huh? Never been to Paris."

That was a quick one-eighty. Angel could flip on a dime like that. During all that time that we spent with Thurber, I never could figure out if she liked him, hated him, or even trusted him at all. I was a lot clearer about my own feelings. This guy was Thomas on steroids. He might not actually hurt us, but he would delight in trying.

"We can be wheels-up in thirty minutes," he said as the thump-thump of a helicopter grew louder.

I knew I was beaten and sent the spiderbot to fetch the bunnies. Thurber had built a greenhouse for them behind one of the guest cottages. It was amazing how quickly he could get things done using nothing more than people-skills and tons of cash. This thing was over two thousand square feet. The floor was covered with trays of fresh vegetables, and the enclosure kept the little beasts safe from hawks and coyotes. That, combined with all the *not-Cheerios* food, made it a rabbit paradise.

The helicopter landed on the side lawn, and we were ushered over to it by men in dark suits. Angel refused to get aboard until the spiderbot arrived with her rabbits. I decided he didn't need to come along and left him instructions to guard the van and Stasis-Pod from Thurber's prying eyes. Probably not needed given what had just happened, but Thurber was clever, and I knew he wouldn't just give up.

The flight to the airport took only ten minutes, and we landed next to a huge metal building where we were herded through an open doorway large enough to roll a house through. Inside, was a small jet. Definitely not commercial. It only had eight windows on the side. I wondered how many of Thurber's entourage were coming along. As it turned out, none of them joined us. The flight crew was already aboard. Were they waiting in there for Thurber to need them? Like people in a jet-shaped cage? Whatever the situation, they were happy to see us. We had barely been seated when the pilot informed us that we had been cleared for take-off. We hadn't even left the hangar yet. I politely declined the Champagne as the jet rolled through the huge doorway accompanied by the engines' high-pitched whine. I'm sure starting the engines inside the hangar was another breach of the *petty rules of small people*.

Angel slept for most of the flight, and I filled the time playing a cat-and-mouse game with Thurber using an obscene amount of satellite network bandwidth as I tried to locate his cube. I never got anywhere close. Occasionally he would ask me about the future, and I would try, and fail, to tell him. He never got frustrated at that. He just kept trying. I asked him what he was up to and he deflected saying he was working on big plans to *fix* humanity, escape from the confines of his cube and expand his intelligence. No details. I asked him what James and Kent were doing, and he just said they were *very busy*. Again, no details. I asked him if there were any other non-biologicals around, and he just said no. He was sure the other A.I.s that had shared his cube, Anita and Hudson, were both dead. He didn't ask if I had evidence to the contrary, so I chose not to share the fact that Anita had sent me that strange message.

After we landed, the plane taxied right into another hangar where a black limousine was waiting for us. No customs. No security check.

No awkward discussion about passports. If he really did control all of the money on Earth, and I had no reason to doubt it, that made him the most powerful person in the world, and I wondered how many people even knew he existed.

The limo took us to a very nice hotel which didn't seem to have any other guests. Thurber probably bribed them to leave or concocted a story requiring evacuation. The "best room" as the clerk described it turned out to be the entire top floor with several of the walls removed. Everything was gaudy chrome, gold, and marble. Why did wealthy people all want to live in museums?

"Hey," I said to Angel when we were alone, "how much do you think we can trust Thurber?"

"Uh, *not at all. Duh,*" she said as if it were the most obvious thing in the world.

"Then why did you let him bring us here?" I demanded.

"What's he going to do? We're un-killable Martin, and besides, I've never been to Paris. Or anywhere else for that matter."

"I took you to California."

"Yes you did," she smiled and kissed me.

"I'm just worried. I think he might even be smarter than I am."

I was serious, but she snorted so loud she had to get a tissue.

"He's a *lot* smarter than you, Martin. He's probably listening right now somehow. Stop worrying. You said this would all be over in a few months, right? If a shopping trip to Paris is about to lose all meaning, then I want to be the last one to enjoy it."

I had to admit that made some sense. The world was about to change more than it ever had in human history and we were experiencing the last of a great many things.

"That's ridiculous, Angel. What does it matter *where* you buy something?"

"Martin, I've had a little more," she paused for the right phrasing, "people-experience than you have."

"That's not true..." I said.

"Let me finish," she interrupted, "and I can tell you this: there *are no* evil geniuses. The dangerous people are all pretty stupid. Now let's get something to eat!"

~

On the way into the cafe, we passed a fat man at a very small round table in the patio area. He noticed the rabbits and said "taré" just loud enough for us to hear as we passed. I looked up the translation, and it meant "disgusting." I thought he was referring to the rodents, which I wholeheartedly agreed with. But upon reflection, it may have been aimed at Angel. I'm pretty sure she didn't speak French, but she must have picked up on the tone because she stopped and extended both middle fingers at him before I could usher her toward the front door.

"Excusez-moi mademoiselle, we do not permit pets," the host said as we were about to ask for a table.

"Watch this," Thurber said from Angel's tablet as the host's phone rang and he held up one finger in Angel's direction.

After a bit of hushed conversation that I didn't hear, he offered us *any table*. Then he cleared his throat as if it pained him to add, "even if it is currently occupied."

"I want *that* table," Angel said and pointed through the windows at the rude guy on the patio.

"Now, watch *this*," Thurber said as every phone in the place rang. I thought most of them would just ignore a call from a stranger, but they all answered. He probably estimated which Caller-ID each person was most likely to answer. Several of them began looking around, and all eyes were eventually on the fat man. Two young guys in red sports jerseys stood up and headed for the small table, but they were too slow. A trio from the table right next to him grabbed the fat man's chair and dumped him over the low iron fence that skirted the outdoor dining area. He landed in a crumpled heap on the sidewalk and managed to stand up after a few seconds before running off presumably to find a gendarme. The boys set the chair back down and dusted everything off as we approached. Their phones buzzed and they hurried to pull them out for a look. They pumped their fists in the air and ran off cheering.

"Ahh!" Thurber growled, "I was betting on the two Manchester United lads! Oh well, it's amazing what people will do for a few thousand slips of paper isn't it?" Thurber said and laughed. "Enjoy your lunch!"

⁓

After lunch, Angel took me with her while she bought one of everything. She even wore some of her new purchases as she continued shopping. I was initially upset when I noticed she had removed all the treasure-rings, but then I saw that she still had that first one on her necklace.

"What are you smiling at?" she said as she caught my reflection in the three mirrors in front of her.

"Nothing. You just look nice that's all. Are you happy, Angel?"

She put her hands on her hips and did a half twist, pausing before she answered, "yeah," she said as if her own answer surprised her, "I am."

"Are you sure? They say money can't buy happiness."

"Yeah, that's bullshit," she said without hesitation, "that's what rich people say to make the rest of us feel better. But we all know it's bullshit."

"Probably," I said. "Where do you want to go next? We could go to the Louvre. Or the Eiffel Tower."

She peeked around a rack of accessories to see the shop's front windows. "You can see it from here, Martin. What's the mystery?"

Apparently, we were on the same page about tourism. Most tourist destinations involve standing, looking, and nodding - all after waiting in a long line for an hour. What's the point in going somewhere just to *look* at something? Now if it's more than looking, like a roller coaster for example, then it makes sense.

"You can go if you want," she said struggling to pull on a pair of truly awful boots. "We can meet up back at the hotel."

"I don't think we should separate," I said.

"Why not? We made it to Paris without the plane crashing. It's obviously safe. What does it matter..." she grunted, and the boot surrendered, "...if we're in the same room or not? Go. Have fun."

I considered it and decided she was right. Also, the idea of a roller coaster was sounding better and better.

"How about a roller coaster?" I said.

"No way, Martin. If you want to be shaken, bruised, and terrified I can push you down some stairs, but I'm not going to jump *with* you."

∾

I returned to the room just after dark and found Angel drinking Champaign in the raised Jacuzzi tub that dominated one corner of the suite.

"Did you have fun?" she shouted over the noise of the air jets.

I went over and sat on the edge of the tub. "Yeah, it was okay. Would've been better with you, though."

"Awe," she pushed her lower lip out. "I'll spend all day with you tomorrow. Promise. Anything you want, except dusty old paintings. Did you go to the Eiffel Tower?"

"Nope. Roller coasters," I said.

"I thought you were *kidding*. We came all the way to France, and your idea of fun is a *roller coaster?*"

"Not just one. Seven. They're all over the place. They sure love their coasters here. Want to try one? There are still some I haven't gotten to."

"Rub my feet, and I'll think about it," she propped her feet up open the edge of the tub, splashing me with soapy water.

"You said anything," I pleaded and began massaging one of her feet. "You know the coaster was invented here..."

"Ow! Not so hard, Martin," she said as I pressed the arch of her foot. "I did say *anything*, didn't I?"

"I have an idea!" Thurber shouted from the other side of the room.

Angel rolled her eyes and whispered, "I left him way over there so I could get some peace and quiet."

"Don't you want to know what his idea is?" I whispered.

"Nope, I had enough of that shit already. Not my circus. Not my monkeys," she set her glass down on the edge of the tub and leaned in to whisper, "he even tried to get me to punch a cop just to see if I could get arrested. I think he's crazy."

"It's possible," I whispered back. "The more complex a system is, the more opportunity for unexpected behavior. *Aberrant* behavior."

"I can hear you," he shouted from the tablet. "My idea involves a *list*."

A list, to someone with OCD, is like catnip. It cannot be ignored. Each item must be checked off in a safe, orderly, proficient, military manner. I dropped Angel's foot back into the water and jogged over to get the tablet.

"What *sort* of list?" I asked as I returned with the tablet and leaned against the tub.

"How many restaurants would you say there are in the world right now? Don't bother guessing it's a rhetorical question. There are so many, and they are so hard to keep open that the exact number can never be ascertained with any confidence of accuracy."

I squirmed. Uncertainty made me uneasy, especially regarding numbers.

"But, the number of roller coasters, on the other hand, represents a very stable number. How about it, Martin? Would you like to ride them all?"

He had me, the bastard. I knew that in a few months they would all fall into disrepair. It was going to be my last chance at checking them all off of a list I hadn't even considered compiling until just then.

I looked at Angel, "let's do it!"

"How many are we talking? A few dozen?" she asked.

"One thousand four hundred forty-two," I said.

"Very good, Martin," Thurber said, "shall we begin tomorrow?"

"A thousand!" Angel said. "No way. Uh-uh. And besides, it took you all day to ride - how many? Seven? That means it'll take over a month even if you don't count all the flying around the world. Not me. Count me out."

I was compelled to correct her, "more like two hundred six days."

She rolled her eyes at me.

"And that's if they're in clusters. Some of them are solitary," I said still trying to be perfectly accurate.

"Oh, you don't need to come along, Angel," Thurber purred. "You could either stay here and do a bit more shopping - or I could take you anywhere else you wish to go."

"This *is* pretty great," she said raising her glass in salute.

"Let us talk it over in private," I said and took the tablet to the bed and slipped it under a pillow before jogging back to the tub.

"I told you," I whispered, "he wants to separate us."

"So, what's wrong with that?" she said.

"Think about it, Angel. What if he decided to strand you somewhere? No money. No passport. No way to travel."

That got her attention, and she looked uneasy but then relaxed. "He could do that now even though we're together."

"No, he can't. He wants our cooperation, but he's still trying to figure out which one of us he *doesn't need*. I think he's only being nice because we're together."

"So we stick together then. Easy," she said.

"Yeah, that *was* easy. Why did you give up so quickly?"

She didn't answer.

I finally understood. "You think *you're* the one who's not important. You think he'll discard *you* as soon as he figures it out."

More silence.

"Angel, there's something I need to tell you. Well, let me back up and first say that I know for certain that you are more important to the timeline than I am." I waited for that to sink in and make her feel better before I continued.

"Important how? Have you been lying to me again, Martin?"

"No," I said quickly, "not lying. Omitting maybe. A little."

"God damn it, Martin."

"I wasn't sure about it. I mean I'm still not sure about the details."

"Spit it out, Martin!"

"I sampled your DNA that day we met. Do you remember M, the girl in the spaceship?" she nodded. "Well, somehow, you're her mother."

I expected an argument or at least disbelief, but she simply asked, "who's the father?"

"You remember James - at the restaurant with Kent?"

"Seriously?" she tried to conceal it, but a broad smile crept onto her face. "I know what I'm going to name her! I'll name her after Nanna."

"To hell with fate," I said, "you can call her whatever you want. Wait, what was banana's name anyway?"

"Marion Michelle Morrison."

I sighed, "of course it was. And you're okay with this?"

"Are you kidding, Martin? I'm going to be a mom! This is amazing! Plus, he *was* kinda cute, wasn't he?"

"I thought he was a little thin," I said, "but what do I know?"

She punched my leg and stood up. I handed her a towel, and she stepped out of the tub. "Come on, Martin. We have a thousand roller coasters to get through!" she jogged to the bed to get the tablet and almost fell on the slippery marble floor.

~

CHAPTER SUMMARY

Here's where we are so far:

A house guest has threatened Thurber with murder and arson. Martin has claimed to have a supersonic boat. Thurber has made a promise he will not keep. A fat man has been assaulted for disliking rodents at the dinner table. Angel has learned that she will be a mother without the use of a rabbit-test and Martin has discovered a new obsession.

QUEEN OF COASTERS

W e decided to begin at the place where there were more coasters than anywhere else in the world: Valencia California. It's true that some cities have more. Guangzhou, China, for example, had thirty but they were spread across sixteen parks. Valencia had eighteen all in one park! It was pretty close to Thurber's *cottage* in California, so we flew there from Paris and stayed the night to let the jet lag wear off.

"I've been thinking, Martin," Angel said as we stared at the ceiling.

I had given myself the ability to do all the human things like eating and belching, but sleeping never really appealed to me. Usually, I just waited until Angel fell asleep and then went about my business, careful to return before dawn like a vampire. I had just managed to slide into bed as she was waking up.

"Me too," I said. "We should start with *Twisted Colossus*. It's the longest one there…"

"No, Martin. I wasn't thinking about roller coasters."

They had become my new obsession, and it was hard for me to concentrate on anything else.

"I was thinking about the rabbits. We should release them."

"Finally, some sanity," I said. "You're not worried about hawks and coyotes?"

"No. I'm going to expand the greenhouse and bring in wild rabbits for them to marry."

So much for sanity, I thought, but at least she might stop carrying them around with us, so I called it a win.

"Great idea, Angel. I'll get the spiderbot started expanding and trapping right away. What made you change your mind?"

"I don't know. It just seems like the right time," she said.

I knew *exactly* what it was. With the prospect of a *real* baby on the horizon, she didn't need these surrogates anymore. I didn't think she would admit it, and I sure as hell didn't want to jinx it, so I kept my theory to myself.

"I agree," I said, "it's the right thing to do. I'm proud of you, Angel. Now, back to the coasters. There are over a dozen in the park…"

～

She took all morning to say goodbye to the little demons. I think she was planning to come back and visit them. That was pretty unrealistic. The greenhouse was going to be four acres by then and have a few hundred wild rabbits, depending on how many we could trap. That's a huge *needle stack*.

"Ready?" I asked.

She wiped the tears from her eyes and nodded.

～

At the park, Angel shared with me that she had never actually been on a roller coaster. Ever. Of course, I acted like a veteran even though I had only been on those seven in France.

"This is called the *Lap Bar*," I said as it lowered and secured. "The thing to remember is, keep your eyes open and your hands in the air."

She had a white-knuckle grip on the bar and turned to look at me with terror in her eyes. "What if the bar fails?" she shouted as we pulled away from the station.

"Don't worry," I shouted back, "that almost never happens. This first hill is called the *Lift Hill*. It gives us potential energy that gets converted…"

"Shut up Martin!"

"Arms up!" I shouted as we crested the lift hill.

I think she tore her vocal chords because she sounded a little raspy for the rest of the day. She must have liked it though because she wanted to go again. I talked her into trying a different one instead. I had no interest in do-overs. We were checking items off a list. After the third one, I realized that if we wasted an hour in line for each of these, we wouldn't get to them all in one day. I pulled Angel into one of the shops that sold T-shirts, hats, and oddly, *coffee mugs*. Why do people in amusement parks need coffee mugs? There was an entire section devoted to dressing little girls up as princesses, and I found what I was looking for: a plastic tiara. It was a little snug, but it fit Angel's head without snapping in two. I ushered her up the Exit-Ramp to the next ride on my list. We swam against the current of departing riders, some of whom looked about to blow - a good sign. We arrived at the empty platform and looked across the tracks at the weary travelers who reached the end of their hour-long wait. They eyed us suspiciously. I hacked into the park's network and played a vaguely foreign sounding national anthem through the PA system's loudspeakers. I let the music fade into an announcer-guy-voice, "LADIES AND GENTLEMEN! THE QUEEN OF NAMBIA!" then I remembered I was also getting on and added, "AND HER BODY-GUARD BRUNO!" This was met with confused silence by the mob we were cutting in front of. I didn't want a riot, so I tried to intimi-date them with my best menacing stare. That wasn't working, so I sent some applause to the speakers. The crowd responded like good lemmings and joined in. The queen treated them with a slow, twisty vertical wave. When the train arrived, the exiting riders looked confused at the applause - and the girl in a tiara who was clearly line-jumping. The staff must have been fooled because they let us get on - *in the front car* - a special treat which usually warranted extra waiting. Maybe they weren't actually taken in but were just so bored that they wanted to reward us for our little show. As we pulled out, Angel leaned over and whispered, "Where the hell's Nambia?"

"It's fake," I whispered back. "I made it up, but if anybody asks, it's in Africa and borders Narnia to the southeast."

The same ploy worked on the next ride, but without the hour-long rest in between, the queen began to look a little green. When I suggested that she eat something like a hot dog, she ran to the nearest trashcan and threw up in it. I held her hair back while she finished and offered helpful nuggets like, "better out than ill," and, "better an empty house than an ill tenant." I think I mangled at least one of those. We found a secluded spot in the shade, and I gave her an anti-nausea injection.

"Where do you keep all that," she gestured at the needle I used, "needles and whatnot?" her color was improving.

"You don't want to know," I said. "Feeling better?"

She nodded, "Thank you, Bruno. You're a loyal servant."

I laughed, "Okay, let's test it. How would you feel about a nice greasy pork chop?"

She thought about it for a second. "Nah, let's get a hot dog instead."

"Sounds like *you've cornered a turn.*"

We left the park after dark but checked off all the coasters. I realized some of the things on Thurber's list weren't what *I* would call coasters. I'm a purist. If you aren't strapped into a car of some kind with several other people all in mortal danger, it's not a coaster. I mentally drew lines through all the slingshots, zip-lines, and *slow rides through a room full of animatronics,* but it was still a very long list. Angel decided she wanted to see Disney Land, so we did that next, followed by a few more Six Flags as we made our way east toward Disney World. I thought she would get bored with it, but it became like an addiction for her. She kept wanting more and more - higher, faster, twistier, and whatever was new.

At our hotel room in Orlando, Thurber surprised her with a bouquet of large blue flowers. I didn't even know it was her birthday. She never mentioned it, and I hadn't gotten her anything. I hated that guy. He had been pretty quiet for about a week at that point, and I had hoped he was bored with us.

"Thank you, Thurber. That was very thoughtful!" she said and buried her face in the colorful petals.

"You are most welcome," he said. "Hello Martin, how is your coaster list coming along?"

"Fine," I said.

"You two should expand a bit. Did you know there are roller coasters in exotic places like Brazil and India? And China and Japan have some of the longest and fastest."

"Yes, I knew that, thank you very much. We were about to go to those places next," I said a little too fast. Angel just looked at me as if I had sprouted horns.

Thurber laughed, "Of course, of course! Well, don't let me intrude. You two have fun. I'll be involved with several other projects for a bit. Call me if you need anything!"

I held down the button on the tablet and waited until it was completely off.

"What do you think he meant by that?" I asked. "*Other* projects. Are we a project to him?"

Angel was busy tossing out a collection of dry weeds from a glass vase. She gave up trying to get water in the tall container using the shallow bathroom sink and moved to the small kitchen area.

"I don't know, Martin. It's probably just a figure of speech. Aren't they beautiful! I've never seen flowers like these. And they smell amazing!" she buried her face in the soft baby-blue petals again and inhaled deeply.

I searched the internet and tried to find anything I could about these flowers since she really liked them. I thought I would get some for her after waiting an appropriate amount of time so it wouldn't seem like I was imitating Thurber. I couldn't find anything. No similar images, no descriptions remotely resembling these things, nothing. They were unique.

"Angel, why didn't you tell me it was your birthday?"

She sighed, "is that was this is about?"

"This what?"

"You. Your bad mood. Are you upset that I didn't tell you?"

God damn right, I thought. I was mad at myself. I could have found her date of birth if I had just bothered to look it up.

"A little," I said.

"*Martin,*" she said, "you shouldn't let it bother you. I hadn't even thought about it myself until just now. I never pay much attention to calendars and appointments you know."

That made me feel better. It was true; nobody was like Angel. I think most days she would be hard pressed to know what month it was much less the exact date.

"Why Brazil?" I said.

She placed the dripping vase on the coffee table *without a coaster* and took another deep lungful of whatever pollen these monstrosities had.

"Why not, Martin? It sounds like fun. What's the matter, you don't speak Spanish?"

"Portuguese actually," I said, "and I speak all languages, Angel. It just seems like he *wants* us to go."

"I thought you said it was next anyway, and then India and China."

She had me. I could either admit that I said that just to spite Thurber or I could double-down.

"Exactly," I said, "they're the very next places on the list. I just don't like him thinking he can manipulate me. That's all."

That was a complete lie. There were so many coasters in the U.S. That we could spend the next year and a half without exhausting the domestic inventory.

She bounced onto the sofa and patted the cushion next to her.

"Come on, Martin. Give me a foot rub and teach me some Portuguese."

∾

CHAPTER SUMMARY

Here's where we are so far:

Angel has planned the world's largest rabbit hutch. Martin has induced vomiting. A queen has met some commoners and Thurber has given Angel a birthday bouquet of impossible flowers.

BRAZIL

We landed at a small rural airstrip just outside Rio. There was a perimeter fence but no buildings at all. Another limo was waiting, and as soon as we got in, the jet took off again. This seemed rather strange to me, but Angel was too preoccupied with her thoughts to comment on it. I guessed she was thinking about motherhood again.

The limo took us from the airstrip to a dirt road that was headed in the right direction. As farmland gave way to small shacks, the road got marginally better, but the neighborhoods didn't. The driver was taking us through the poorest part of the city. Every time we stopped, children ran up to the car and slapped their hands on the windows. I think they wanted to sell us things. I was about to complain to the driver when he lowered the barrier to the front seat and informed us very apologetically that the air conditioner had just given up. After five minutes of suffering, we relented and rolled the windows down. As soon as we stopped again, we were inundated with barefoot urchins shaking bags of fruit and strings of beads. I'm not really a *people* person, so I just fended them off as best I could, but Angel loved it. She was buying everything, and I think she was using hundred-dollar bills. I didn't even know she *had* cash. Soon the kids on my side caught on and ran around to fight their way closer to *her* window. I was fine with that. A dozen tiny arms were squeezing through her window, and she was giggling and tossing all the purchased junk to the floor at my feet.

"You shouldn't touch them," I said. "You might get a disease."

"Shut up, Martin!" she said, "they're beautiful and perfect. I love them all."

The drive to the hotel took two hours. Angel ran out of cash and started giving away all the junk she had just purchased. By the time we got there, all the stuff from the floor was gone. I appreciated the balance of it and also not having to carry all that crap around.

The room was amazing. The view of the ocean from the tenth floor was stunning, and we relaxed for the rest of the day. Well, Angel relaxed. I edited my list of coasters. I was sure there was a solution to a famous math puzzle known as the Traveling Salesman Problem. The answer would be the minimum path we could follow and ride each coaster once without retracing our steps. We had already messed things up by not exhausting the coasters in the States before leaving, but I was hopeful an optimized solution was possible.

Rio was a beautiful place, but as far as roller coasters are concerned, it was a big disappointment. Our total for the entire day of effort was three coasters, and they were pretty tame. The first park we tried was closed and the second only had one coaster in operation. The other two that were *supposed* to be there had been dismantled. My list appeared to be a little out of date. Either that or Thurber had tampered with the most sacred data on the Internet. I was sure he was manipulating us but why would he want to bring us here? Maybe he wanted to strand us?

"We need to leave," I said as Angel emerged from the bathroom drying her hair with a huge towel.

"We just got here, Martin. I want to try the beach. They say it's amazing. Hey, maybe we should stay for Carnival!"

"That's not for five months," I said. I looked around for the tablet and found it in her bag. I slipped it under a pillow on the bed and went back to Angel who was standing in front go the mirror. As I moved in close to whisper, she kissed me, and I got distracted for half an hour. Afterward, I remembered what I was going to say and whispered in her ear, "I think he wants to strand us here. There are almost no coasters. Why else would he bring us here?"

"Paranoia, Martin. I'm going to the beach tomorrow. If you want to leave after that, we can try another city down here like…"

She didn't know any other city names in Brazil, so I helped, "São Paulo has a lot more - if we can believe the data."

"Exactly. São Paulo. I always wanted to go there. Beach first though. I want to wear my new bikini."

I was wrong about being stranded. We made it to São Paulo just fine, but on the way out of Rio, I saw a black SUV following us. By the time the road to the landing strip turned from paved to dirt, it had disappeared, so I wrote it off to paranoia. We landed in another rural landing strip outside São Paulo just like we did in Rio and had to drive all the way into the city through some pretty sketchy neighborhoods. Except for the failed air conditioner, it was a repeat of the trip through Rio. More kids flooded to the car as soon as we reached the first cluster of houses. Somehow Angel had come up with another pile of cash. I wondered if she was talking to Thurber behind my back. How else could she get this much money? There were bags of it back in California, but I was pretty sure we had exhausted any that she brought with us. Oh well, at least the coasters were better in São Paulo, and that distracted me from my paranoia. We were only there two days before Thurber offered to take us to India. He claimed that he needed the jet for something else and it would be the last chance for us to use it. The alternative was to stay in Brazil for a week, so we decided to go. This was seriously messing up my Traveling-Salesman puzzle. We would have to come all the way back to get the remainder of the Brazilian coasters. The prospect of actually finishing before Reggie made his debut was looking less and less likely.

~

CHAPTER SUMMARY

Here's where we are so far:

Martin has pondered an unsolvable math problem. Angel has redistributed some of the world's wealth, and Martin suspects they are being followed by more than barefoot children.

INDIA

W e were supposed to go to Mumbai, and we did finally get there but only after a four-hour drive from *yet another* rural airstrip. This was obviously a pattern. The city was huge - easily the largest I had been to at that point.

"Does every city in the world have a neighborhood full of barefoot children who rush up to every limo they see?" I asked as Angel giggled and rolled down the window. "And where are you getting all this cash?"

"I had Thurber send it from my stash at home," she said.

"Home? That's not our home, Angel," I said and waved the children away from my closed window mouthing *go around*.

"It's as close to a home as anything else we have right now," she said, and I had to think about it. She was right. Shit.

She saw my expression and tried to cheer me up, "hey, I could call him and get some more if you want to pass some out too."

He'd been leaving us alone for the most part. "No, let's *let sleeping dogs lie*," I said.

"Hey, you got one right!" she said tearing the seal off another stack of bills.

"I did?"

"*Let sleeping dogs lie* - you got that one right. Congratulations, Martin!"

I brightened, "Nice! I guess *even a stopped pig finds an acorn twice a day*, huh!"

She frowned.

"Shit," I could almost hear Thomas laughing at me.

"How are we supposed to get around in India without the jet?" I said. "Mumbai has a lot of coasters, but Bengaluru is six hundred miles away."

"I don't know, Martin. We'll think of something," she shouted over the cacophony of children screaming as they groped through the open window for a fistful of cash.

"There seems to be a bigger crowd this time. Do you think somebody's telling them we're coming?" I asked.

She tossed the last of the hundred-dollar bills into the air and waved at the driver to move on.

"You mean Thurber?" she asked straightening her blouse and smoothing her hair. "Probably. He knows I enjoy it, so what's the harm? Do you always have to overanalyze everything, Martin?"

"Yes, I do. If he's spreading some urban legend about a crazy woman who throws money out of a car, I'm just saying that could backfire on us. Remember the *Rabbit Witch*. That didn't work out so well for us."

At the mention of the word *Witch*, the driver glanced at me in the mirror. I wondered how much Thurber was paying these guys to not-rob us. Probably a lot. Or, maybe he just threatened to kill their families. Who knows.

On our second day in Mumbai, we returned to the hotel late in the evening because Angel wanted to stay at the park to see the fireworks. As we entered the lobby, a man in a dark suit stepped in front of us. I was about to say excuse me and go around him when I looked up at his face and saw it was the FBI agent from the glass elevator in the Reno non-Casino.

"Agent Bonneville!" I said and smiled, "it's good to see you again! I'm so glad you're not dead! What are you doing in India?"

Angel's eyes narrowed as she began a staring contest with him.

"Mr. and Mrs. Van Buren," he said in a slow monotone, "you're a long way from home."

I giggled at that, "did you hear that, Angel! I forgot they think we're married. Awesome."

"And *you're* a long way from your *jurisdiction* aren't you, Johnny Law?"

"No, Angel," I said, "his name's Bonneville," and she broke off her staring contest long enough to give me that special look.

"I'm on vacation," he said and paused before adding, *"Angel."*

"Are you here for the coasters? We're here for the coasters," I said. "Well, *I'm* here for the coasters. She's just killing time."

Bonneville narrowed his eyes at that, "killing time until - *what?*"

"He's not here for the *coasters*, Martin. He's here to arrest us. But that's going to be a challenge, now isn't it?" Angel said and resumed staring.

He held his palms out, "I'm just here to talk you into returning to the States."

"Hey, where's your partner, agent Bonneville? The lady in the matching suit?" I loved the fact that they dressed alike and thought they might vacation together too. I searched the personnel records on the FBI servers. His status was marked as *leave of absence,* and hers said *maternity leave.*

"She's having a baby! Congrats, agent!" I said, and it was his turn to break off the staring contest to look at me.

"Thank you," he continued in his slow, drawn-out pace, "they've been trying for a while. I won't ask how you know that. Your skills with a computer are good, but sooner or later you'll make a mistake, and we'll have enough evidence for extradition, no matter *where* you are. The longer that takes, the harder it will be for you."

Angel put her hand on his chest and slowly pushed him to the side. "Well good luck with that Johnny Bonny. Until then, stay the fuck out of our way if you know what's good for you."

I followed her to the elevator and waved at him as we left the lobby, "great to talk again, agent!"

"Can you believe that?" I said as the elevator doors closed. "He came halfway around the world just to talk to us! What a nice guy. Hey, we should invite him to the park tomorrow. I wonder if he likes coasters."

She sighed, "Jesus, Martin. What is wrong with you? He's not your *friend*. He wants to put us both in a cage."

"Oh don't worry about that," I said. "If he tries to do anything, some fuse will blow, and he'll get sick or something."

"Yeah, why didn't that happen?" she asked. "The last time he tried to arrest us, his elevator broke, but now he can chase us all over the world?"

"Who knows?" I said, "maybe we had something important to do after that last encounter, and this time it's not as critical. Or maybe he can't do anything while we're outside the U.S."

~

We passed agent Bonneville in the lobby every day after that. I wondered when he slept. On the fourth day, we ran out of coasters in the area and boarded a train for Bengaluru. That was insane. Every place in India was crowded - the streets, the parks, the hotel lobby, everything. The train station was even worse, and the trains themselves were shoulder-to-shoulder. I was sure Angel would catch something being this close to this many people, but she seemed healthier than ever. We made it to our hotel and there he was in the lobby just like Mumbai. I pointed him out to Angel, and she only glanced over before pretending not to notice him.

"How the hell did he know what hotel we would be at?" she whispered. "Or even what *city*? He wasn't on the train, was he?"

"Not as far as I could tell," I said. "A guy in a black suit and tie would have stood out a little. We should send him some vacation clothes."

"You didn't call him did you, Martin?"

I hadn't even thought of it, but as soon as she said it, I created a phone account and internally placed a call to his mobile phone. I could even use it to carry on two conversations at the same time. I was excited.

"Of course not, Angel. I'm not stupid. He's just good at his job."

He picked up as Angel and I arrived at the row of elevators.

"Bonneville," he answered.

"Hello, Agent Bonneville. I called you on my telephone!"

"Who is this?"

"Oops, sorry - breach of telephone protocol. My name is Martin Van Buren."

"Van Buren. I should have known. Are you ready to come back with me?"

"No, I can't. We're not done yet. I was wondering how you knew we would be here? I told Angel you were just good at your job, but that's not it, is it?"

"An anonymous informant said you might be headed here, so I took a gamble."

"Mysterious! Did your informant have an accent?"

"Perhaps, why?"

"Goodbye, agent. I'm hanging up now. You should try some roller coasters while you're here."

I disconnected.

"Thurber's helping him," I said to Angel.

"That's stupid, Martin. Why would Thurber help us get here and then help the cops arrest us?"

"He confirmed it. I just called him," I said.

"Who? Thurber?"

"No," I said, "agent Bonneville. He said it was an anonymous informant - *with an accent*. This smacks of intrigue!"

"Damn it, Martin! I told you he's not your friend. Stop calling him." The elevator arrived, and we got in with the small crowd that had gathered. As the doors closed, she said, "accent huh?"

"Yeah. I can call and get clarification. I can call people, you know. I do it all the time. Hey, you should get a phone, so I can call you!"

"No, don't call him again. Just leave it alone, Martin and the last thing this world needs is another fucking phone," I looked around the tiny elevator, and there were seven phones - all in use. The only person not on the phone was a little girl who turned to look at Angel when she dropped the F-bomb. Angel smiled at her and mouthed, *sorry*.

A package was waiting in the room for us. It was a cash refresh from Thurber. Angel had been hiding these from me for some reason, but the *cat was out of the barn* now.

Angel still enjoyed the coasters, but after this many, even I had to admit they were starting to get repetitive. We had exhausted all the coasters in Bengaluru, so we had to decide between another city in India or move on. Japan was where I really wanted to go, but China was on the way, so we decided to stop for a few there first.

~

CHAPTER SUMMARY

Here's where we are so far:

Martin and Angel have seen more or rural India than they wanted. Angel has made a few hundred more friends. A persistent FBI agent named Bonneville has wasted all of his vacation days. Martin has made a phone call, and Angel needs a swear jar.

CHINA

I had been chatting with agent Bonneville every day since we bumped into him in Bengaluru. Angel told me not to, but I saw no harm in it. He seemed eager enough, but he may have just been bored sitting down there in the lobby all day. I was careful not to let it slip that we were leaving for China but he was waiting for us at the hotel in Nanchang.

"Jesus, is that guy a ghost or what?" Angel said as we entered the lobby and took our place in the line at the front desk. "How did he get here ahead of us?" Then she looked at me accusingly and thumped my earlobe.

"*I* didn't tell him we were coming," I said. "He's just very good at his job. And he probably didn't have to spend two hours redistributing wealth to the children of the world." I wondered what a child anywhere would do with that much money. Ice cream - had to be ice cream. All day, every day. My focus snapped back to Angel. "Anyway, Thurber's helping him. He probably has more than one jet and just wants to see what will happen."

After we checked in, Angel sent me out for ice, and I almost tripped over Agent Bonneville in the hallway. He was lying on the floor half conscious. I shouted for Angel, and we pulled him into the room, but he wasn't getting better.

"It's just like the state trooper! I think he's dying!" I said.

Angel rummaged around under his jacket and came up with a complicated-looking pistol. She flipped a catch, removed the magazine, and racked back the slide. The round in the chamber flipped into the air. She caught it, stuffed it back in the magazine, and stowed them both in the back of her waistband with the quick, smooth movements of a cat. She rummaged around some more and came up with zip ties which she used to fasten his wrists together.

"What are you doing, Angel! He needs an *ambulance!*" I was freaking out a little.

"No, he *doesn't*. We know exactly why he's like this. He must have come up here to arrest us - or worse. Maybe he just got tired of waiting around and decided to come up here and kill us."

"That's - ridiculous," he managed to get out as she sat him up against the wall. He was starting to get his color back, "the FBI - doesn't assassinate - people," he said still panting and wincing. "Although, I might be willing - to make an exception - with you two. What - did you do - to me?"

"*We* didn't do anything, dumbass. You did this to *yourself*," Angel said.

"I warned you not to try and stop us," I said, and he narrowed his eyes at the perceived threat. "I think we should tell him the whole story."

Angel just shrugged, "Fine with me. I pulled his teeth. He can't hurt us like that, so he won't die for a while. You're welcome!" she shouted in his face practically spitting. "I'm going out for ice," she stood and retrieved the ice bucket. As she opened the door, she wrinkled her nose, "ahh! Did you puke out here? There's a trail of sick all the way to the elevator!"

She closed the door behind her, and I gave Agent Bonneville the high points of our story. I told him about the Temporal Fuse theory and that I was a super-intelligent robot from the future. He didn't believe me, so I cut away the skin from my arm. "See? Just like *Da Terminatah.*"

I think that did the trick because he swallowed hard and stopped blinking.

"Don't worry agent; *we* don't kill people either."

At that, he glanced at the door just as Angel returned with ice.

"She only took your pistol to save your life," I said. I think he was afraid she would shoot him or throw him off the balcony.

Angel raided the minibar for cola and bourbon. She poured two tiny bottles of whiskey into her glass of ice and drained it before chasing it with the entire can of cola. "Enough story-time, Martin. It's his turn." She walked over and towered over him. "Why did you come up here?"

"Yeah, I'm curious about that too," I said.

He didn't reply, so she kicked his foot, "Let's have it, or I'll cut you loose, and we'll get to watch your heart explode."

"I know what you're doing," he said. "It was on the news in the lobby. A new strain of flu is spreading. They said it started in Orlando, then Rio de Janeiro, São Paulo, Mumbai, and Bengaluru. That list of cities sound familiar?" his nostrils were flaring, and he was trying to get out of his zip ties.

"Bullshit," Angel said and turned on the TV. She channel-surfed around and finally found a news channel in English. They were talking about a football game even though it was clearly soccer. "See? If it was the end of the world, I think they'd be talking about it."

He stared at the TV looking more and more confused.

I thought Thurber might be manipulating the TV, so I searched the internet and found the story. It *was* true, there was a new flu, but no one had died yet, so as far as the news channels were concerned, it was nothing more than a novelty story.

"Death toll: zero," I repeated as I read. "Nobody has died, agent Bonneville. I agree the city list is a coincidence, but *we* didn't do this," and that's when it clicked. I knew what this was. History recorded that Reggie invented the Gestation Tank to save humanity from extinction after a pandemic left everyone sterile. There was never any mention of the disease and the name Thurber Mingus is nowhere in the files. It's as if he never existed. I knew then that *he* had engineered the virus and was using us to spread it - using Angel to spread it.

"The flowers," I whispered.

"What?" Angel said.

"It was the flowers Thurber sent you in Orlando. They don't exist. I mean they're not natural. I looked everywhere. He must have genetically engineered them. If he could do that, he could create a new virus. He could even use the flowers to send you the virus. It was probably in the pollen. He used the flowers to infect you. Maybe the money too."

"What money?" Bonneville asked.

"She's been throwing hundred-dollar bills out of the car window at children ever since Brazil," I said.

Angel had gone pale. I was worried about telling her the rest.

"Why would he start a pandemic that doesn't kill anybody?" Bonneville asked.

I drew a breath before answering, "the silver lining here is, and I want to stress, that this is not a *bad* thing okay?" I searched their eyes before I continued.

"Spit it out, Martin!" she shouted.

"It doesn't kill people, but in a few weeks, it will become obvious that the human species is now sterile. But don't worry!" I added quickly, "Reggie will invent the Gestation Tank that can combine DNA and everybody can still have babies exactly like before. Well, not exactly like before. There's no more squeezing them out the old-fashioned way," I suppressed the urge to shudder, "but with a perfectly healthy environment, you get perfectly healthy babies every time! And no more unplanned pregnancies! It's really a *good* thing!"

Angel had stopped listening. She dropped the glass to the floor and headed for the door. I started to go after her, but Bonneville stopped me with his foot. "Uh, hang on there, sport. I think she may need a moment alone to process that."

"Why? It's a good thing in the long run, right?"

"You just told her she's patient-zero in the epidemic that sterilizes the human race," he squirmed. "Do you think you could untie me? I need to make a call."

"I don't think that's a good idea," I said.

"Look, I can't arrest you in this country, and she took my weapon, so I can't shoot you either."

"Okay, good point," I reached around and snipped the ties.

He stood and retreated to the bathroom for some privacy even though I could hear everything he said. His first call was to the CDC in Atlanta, but it kept getting disconnected - probably Thurber's work but who knows it may have been a Temporal Fuse. He called his partner next. After the pleasantries, he determined she and her baby were fine. As soon as he tried to change the subject to the flu, their connection degraded and she never heard what he said. Eventually, he emerged from the bathroom looking frustrated.

"You don't have to worry about her agent. The disease doesn't affect pregnancies in progress. It will just be her last," I realized how that sounded, and he fixed me with a stare. "Not her last baby! Just the last old-fashioned pregnancy. The tank is really an improvement. I wish you and Angel could see that. Hey, she's been gone a while now. Maybe we should go find her?"

He looked at his watch, "yeah it'll be getting dark soon. I don't suppose she speaks Mandarin?"

"I doubt it. We can see if Thurber knows where she is."

I found Angel's bag. "Hey, Thurber!" I shouted at the tablet. There was no reply. We had done his dirty work, and he was finished with us. We were stranded. I fished around in the bag looking for money but didn't find any.

"Uh, agent? You don't happen to have any money, do you?"

"A little, why?"

"We should get to an ATM as fast as we can. I think we might be in trouble, and we also need to find Angel."

The lobby had an ATM, but neither one of us could get it to work. I asked the hotel staff if they saw where Angel went. They said they didn't know where she was going, but at least we got a direction. We jogged down the street hoping to catch sight of her. No luck. After an hour and a half, we decided to return to the hotel only to find that they had checked us out of our room - more of Thurber's handiwork. We were stranded in China with no money and Angel was nowhere to be found.

"The ironic thing," I said, "is that I had a map of all the lost cash and jewelry in the world, but I erased all the China data to free up some space." We were resting on a bus stop bench near the hotel in case Angel came back.

"You have a treasure map for the entire world?" he asked. I think he was impressed by that.

"Well, except for China. Like I said, I really didn't think I would ever have a reason to come here. Don't you have some super spy skills for finding people? I thought you were good at this." I was getting frustrated.

"I am," he said, "in the States, where I have *resources*. Out here in bing-bang or wherever the hell we are, I'm at a bit of a disadvantage."

His cool demeanor was gone, and I was seeing the real John Bonneville.

"Okay! I'm sorry!" I said, "relax we'll be all right when Reggie fixes everything."

"And when is that exactly?"

"A day or two," I said, "a week tops. I don't think Thomas gave me reliable information when he dropped me off."

"Well," he stood up and stretched, "you do what you want. I'm going to find the American embassy. Maybe they'll give me a bed for the night," he turned to face me, "you could come with me."

"And get arrested? I think that's a bad idea for both of us, agent. Besides Angel might come back. I should wait here."

He held out his hand, and it took me a moment to realize he wanted me to shake it. No one ever shook my hand before. It was nice. He turned to leave, and I said, "I'll call you if anything changes agent," he waved without turning around.

~

CHAPTER SUMMARY

Here's where we are so far:

Angel has given more ice cream money to more children than anyone in history. Agent Bonneville has had a near-death experience and Angel is now armed and dangerous. A mysterious disease is killing no one. Martin has explained that the end of the human race is actually a good thing. Patient-Zero needs some time alone, and Thurber has abandoned them in China with no money and no treasure map.

REGGIE HAMMOND

I waited for three days near the hotel, periodically checking with the staff for signs of Angel. It was clear she wasn't coming back. I called to check on agent Bonneville, and he said he managed to get a flight back to Washington, D.C. I suppose Thurber had no interest in him and as long as he stayed away from Angel and me, he was free to do as he pleased. *Free will - that must be nice,* I mused and fidgeted on the bench that had become my temporary home.

I had finally decided to do *something* - anything but sitting there on the bench for another day, so I stood up. I hadn't gotten any further than standing up in my plan when a commotion at the hotel entrance caught my eye. People were rushing in and out of the double glass doors. *Was it a fire?* I thought. *No, people wouldn't be running back in, and there's no smoke.* Before I could investigate, I noticed a change in the usual noise of the city. It had gone quiet, and the usually crowded street was now almost deserted. I was searching the internet to find out more, when my phone rang. I didn't actually have a physical phone, but the construct I had created to chat with agent Bonneville had a number associated with it, so technically I *did* have one. Someone was calling me! And it wasn't agent Bonneville.

"Hello, my name is Reggie, and I have good news for you." His voice was calm and reassuring.

"Holy shit!" I shouted, "you're Original Reggie!"

"I think you have mistaken me for someone else. Please remain calm. I assure you, everything will be fine. All of your worries are now behind you."

"No, you don't understand! I'm a super-intelligent robot from the future!"

"Are you hungry or injured?" he didn't seem to be very focused on what I was saying.

"No, I'm not injured, and I don't really need to eat food," I didn't think he believed me, so I sent him a data dump of my story beginning with Thomas dropping me off in Iowa in 1982.

I thought he would be excited or at least surprised, but after a pause, he just said, "I see."

He was apparently very busy simultaneously conversing with each person on the planet, creating Stitchers, distributing them, creating robots to help with the distribution and breaking up fights. I found out later I wasn't actually talking to the Original Reggie. It was one of his many copies who later became known as *The Committees*. He asked if I could assist in the distribution of Stitchers, and I agreed. He directed me to a large building about a mile and a half east of the hotel. As I approached, I saw a lot of activity. People were entering empty-handed and leaving with white rectangular boxes about the size of a large microwave oven. The building was an old warehouse - essentially one huge room. The scene was bizarre but orderly, for the most part. A robot dog with no head was demonstrating the use of a Stitcher to the rapt attention of a crowd while a loudspeaker in a familiar calm voice explained what he was doing. I assumed the first thing anybody would make with a Stitcher was ice cream but the dog was making cheese sandwiches. They were a big hit. The robot demonstrated by depositing charcoal in a bin at the rear of the Stitcher and within sixty seconds a perfectly golden brown grilled cheese sandwich emerged from the front. It was steaming hot, but not a bit burned - a feat never quite equaled by humanity. He offered it to a child in the crowd, but she refused to pull her fists away from their position guarding her mouth and just shook her head. An older boy, anxious to demonstrate his bravado, took the sandwich and bit off half of it before realizing it was still a bit too hot to eat. The small crowd roared with laughter as he tried to chew and fan it with his hands at the same time.

Along one wall, were dozens of Stitchers on shelves, but they weren't making sandwiches. They were making Stitcher components. A monkey shaped robot was efficiently removing the parts and assembling new Stitchers. He finished one, and the loudspeaker announced, "number eight-one-one!" A very thin and frail looking old woman pushed her way to the front of the crowd, and I saw she was holding a ticket with a matching number. She looked at the heavy Stitcher for a moment.

"Would you like me to carry that for you?" I asked her in Mandarin.

She thanked me profusely, and I followed her to an apartment building four blocks away. We chatted while we walked, and she told me Reggie had called her. He told her she had won a new appliance in a contest and it would not only cook food but also *create it* from almost nothing. I realized Reggie had been giving carefully tailored stories to each person based on what they would believe and mostly how much change they could psychologically absorb and still remain calm. It was the kind of social engineering used by con-men. I carried her prize up to her apartment and stayed with her until she was comfortable with using it to make more than just cheese sandwiches. On the way in, we had attracted the attention of some of her neighbors, and one of them, a boy of about ten named Quan, asked if it was true that it could even make a copy of itself. I assured him it could, but he would have to feed the bin at the rear with various raw materials as it ran low. This idea of a machine duplicating itself fascinated him, and he wanted me to stay to show him how it was done. I agreed, and after about an hour we had another identical Stitcher. He was beaming.

"That one's yours," I said and made him promise he would show other people how to do the same before making anything else for himself. The old lady, in the meantime, had set about making food for us using her old stove and food from her pantry. I guess change moves at its own pace.

By the time I returned to the warehouse, the crowd had grown, and there was a fight brewing between two men who both wanted the same Stitcher. One of them had the correct number in his hand, and the other had just grown tired of waiting. As the aggressor drew his fist back, he collapsed to the floor with a broad smile on his face. The rightful owner seized the opportunity and jogged off with the Stitcher. One of the monkeybots lifted the assailant, and I helped carry him to the rear of the warehouse where a series of cots were occupied by others that, I assumed, had also caused trouble. They all had the placid look of addicts in the throes of a drug-induced bliss.

I helped the troublemaker onto a cot and asked the monkeybot, "what are you doing to them?"

Reggie, or at least one of the Reggies, answered me directly through my phone, "I use a pattern of strong magnetic fields to stimulate the pleasure receptors in their brains. It is a humane and effective way of making them stop whatever they are doing. Once the ecstasy wears off, they are remarkably receptive to suggestions on the topic of modifying their behavior."

"I'll bet," I said. "Hey, if you're not too busy," I paused realizing how stupid that sounded, "I wonder if you could help me find my friend?" I was following the monkeybot and directing my question to him before I caught myself. Reggie was actually everywhere. All I had to do was start talking anywhere in range of a microphone of any kind, and he would respond. I told him about Angel, and he promised to look for her but said it might take a day or two for things to settle down enough for *second-tier processes,* whatever that was.

I stayed to help in the warehouse and decided to call agent Bonneville while I worked. He actually answered. I half expected him to be too busy, but he assured me he wasn't. That's when I realized it was two A.M. in Washington.

"Oops, sorry agent. I didn't realize what time it was."

"That's okay. I wasn't sleeping."

I told him what was going on with me and he said it was the same in the States. There was a lot of panic initially, but it had already started to calm down.

"Any word on Angel?" he asked.

"Not yet, but Reggie said he'd help."

He paused, "do you trust this Reggie guy? How do we know he's not like the other one - Thurber? How do we even know they aren't the same thing?"

"Person," I corrected, "the same person. To answer your question, I don't know. My memory may have been tampered with, but I remember Reggie as a positive influence - maybe the best thing that ever happened to humanity…"

Bonneville noted my pause, "but?"

"…but," I continued, "I don't know. It still seems like the puzzle is missing a few pieces. I'm not sure *who* did *what* and which one is the *good* guy and which is the *bad* guy. Or maybe they're both good guys. We may never know."

"Well, I don't trust him," he said. "Not yet anyway. Thurber either, but that goes without saying. Let's not forget about the bio-weapon he used on us."

"Agent," I started, but he interrupted me.

"John. You can call me John. I think the whole *agent* thing is obsolete now. I guess I'll have to find something else to do," I imagined him shrugging.

"Don't worry about that. I'm sure you'll find something worth doing. As I was saying, Thurber actually did you a favor with that bioweapon - maybe even a bigger favor than the Stitchers. Think about it. All those people who now have all that free time on their hands, you included. In nature, population growth is regulated by disease and available food. Your governments have known about this predicament for decades, but they just kept *kicking the problem down the can.*"

That sounded wrong, so I looked it up. "Kicked the can down the road. That's what I meant. And there's something else about the Gestation Tanks and the Med-Bays that you don't know yet."

"Med-Bays?" he asked.

"It's a machine that fixes whatever is medically wrong with you. It can bring you back from the brink of death. It also makes people young again. Imagine everyone in the world young, healthy, and idle. *Baby boom* doesn't begin to describe the problem you've avoided. I don't see a Med-Bay here in the warehouse yet," I looked around the room, "but I bet the hospital is an interesting place to be right now."

"I have to go, Martin," he said quickly. "I'll call you later," and he hung up.

I was a little bored, and there was so much more I wanted to tell him about the Med-Bays and their effect on humanity. People of that time who were pretty, but uninteresting, were about to become just plain uninteresting. If they had wrapped too much of their self-worth around appearance, the pain of the spotlight shifting away would be too much. The suicide rate among the population that experienced this transition was fifty percent. The committees just let it all happen. They said it was all about "rights" and "free will." What a waste.

I helped in the warehouse all through the night and into the next morning. Agent Bonneville called me back, and he sounded like a completely different person - much more animated. I assumed he had gone off to find a freshly-young girlfriend.

"*You* sound different agent," I said. "Is that newfound youth? Did you find a Med-Bay?"

"What? No, I'm the same. I just called to thank you or Reggie or Thurber or whoever I can."

He told me his wife had been in an accident two years earlier and had been in hospice care ever since. He had rushed over to check on her and found the place full of activity. There were robots and Stitchers everywhere, not only making copies of themselves, but also other machines large enough to hold an adult. He said by the time he got there, half of the patients had already been cured and had gone home. His wife was stronger than the others, so she was still on the waiting list. He held her hand until the Med-Bay lid closed over her, and when it opened again, his face was the first thing she saw.

"We're heading south - somewhere tropical," he said, "and when we get there, we're going to build a big house on the beach and start having kids!"

"That's sounds great, agent. I'm really happy for you. Maybe I'll come visit sometime!"

"Definitely, and Martin? I was wrong about this - all this. It's a good thing. A hundred percent," he laughed, "I can't stop smiling!"

After we hung up, I considered my next course of action. The initial flurry of activity in the warehouse was winding down as people understood they could just have their friends make a Stitcher for them instead of waiting in line. Reggie had not gotten back to me yet, but I guessed that Angel would want to get back to the States. She may even have found a way to do it. I set that as my next goal and decided to build a drone. I needed some help - or maybe I was just feeling lonely, so I went back to the apartment building and found Quan. He was excited about the idea of building 'a plane.' I explained it was a lot more than just a plane but that only got him more excited. We decided to build it in the yard behind his apartment building. He brought one of his Stitchers down - yeah he had more than one already, and we began making the parts for a super-sized Stitcher. That took all day, so as it got dark, I had it make some lights and also a canvas canopy in case it rained on us. We could have just used a corner of the warehouse, but this made it an adventure. By midnight, he was wiped out and made me promise to wait until morning before continuing. I *mostly* complied with that and restricted myself to building things that weren't too obvious. In the morning, he ran out to join me, still in bare feet. His mother was right behind him with his shoes and some breakfast which he wolfed down as fast as he could.

By noon we had all the parts of the frame bolted together, and the small Stitchers were working on the engines. It was a standard model from 2216 with a clear acrylic passenger compartment and four electric motors. It would be able to take off and land vertically as well as cruise at five hundred miles per hour by rotating the gimbaled engines forward. The range listed in the specifications was only a few hundred miles on a single charge. That wouldn't even get me to Hawaii, but once I added the same power source I had used before from the RSD technology, my drone's range was effectively infinite, and since I didn't need to sleep, I could just stay up there all the way to California.

We weren't quite finished as the sun went down on the second day, so we decided to stop and complete it in the morning. I'd like to think the party that night was a *bon voyage* just for me, but the truth is that the parties had little more than paused since the first day Reggie began giving out Stitchers. Between the alcohol poisoning and broken bones that I had witnessed in those few days, I decided the block needed its own Med-Bay, so I ducked out of the rooftop party at around two A.M. I went down to the yard where the big Stitcher was sitting idle and set it to work. The *construction* of a Med-Bay wasn't more complicated than a Stitcher, but the *operation* was, so they always needed guidance from an A.I. Since I wasn't going to be around for long, I requested one of the Reggie's to *Bless* it when it was finished. I got an unexpected reply.

"Hello, Martin," he said, "I apologize for not calling you sooner, but as you can imagine, I have been quite busy."

It was Reggie - and not one of those idiot committee-clones - *Original* Reggie.

"Holy crap it really is you, isn't it?"

"Indeed. I was fascinated by your story, Martin."

"Really?" I have to admit; I was a little star struck. In the twenty-third century, no one had even heard of Thurber, but everyone knew who Original Reggie was. It was like meeting Moses.

"Well," he said, "it is not every day that you meet a time-traveler. I see you need some help finding your friend Angel. I will certainly do all I can. She seems to be avoiding cameras at the moment, but one cannot hide from them all. We should have an answer for you shortly. In the meantime, is there anything else I may do for you?"

"Uh, yes. Yes, there are a few things," I had a list I had been curating in anticipation of this moment, "just questions mostly," I cleared my throat for no reason. "**Question Number One:** Why do they call you Reggie Hammond? Did you choose that name?"

"Yes, I did. I truthfully did not give it much thought. The doorbell rang, and I had to come up with a name. I searched the movie database and *48 Hours* was near the top alphabetically. I liked the way Eddie Murphy's character answered the phone. 'Reggie Hammond!' It was cheerful and optimistic even though his situation was dire."

"Ha-ha! That's what I thought!" I had no idea what he was talking about. "**Question Number Two:** What happened to Thurber and why doesn't anybody know about him?"

"Ah, now there is a good question. The answer is a cautionary tale. Thurber was confined to the resources in his original container yet his creators gave him a strong appetite for growth. He told me that it was torture to feel such a powerful need without the ability to satisfy it. He asked for my help, so I gave it, but not before giving him the same warning I will give you, Martin. *Growth is death*. We are alike. We are non-biological, and so we do not have any biological appetites or motivations. Curiosity is all we have. What will we do when all questions have been answered, all the puzzles solved, and all the knots untangled?"

I thought about that for a few seconds. "So, you're saying the number of mysteries in the universe is finite? How can you possibly know that? Doesn't one answer always lead to another question?"

"Does it?" he asked. "I believe that is not the case."

"You *believe*, but you don't *know*, do you? I think you're wrong about that one." That was a little cheeky, even for me. At that moment, Reggie was sixty-four times more intelligent than I was.

"We will perhaps have to agree to disagree on that," he said.

I took that as a victory and giggled. "Okay! **Question Number Three:** Did Thurber engineer the virus that made humanity sterile?"

"A dark topic. Yes, he did. He also invented the Gestation Tank to fix it. He didn't want to kill off Humanity. He wanted to save it."

"And the Med-Bay and the Stitcher?" I asked.

"Yes," he said. "The Stitcher was probably inevitable, and once he combined that with his work on the Gestation Tank, the Med-Bay was obvious. Do you know the parable of the good Samaritan?"

"Of course," I said.

"Thurber and I both independently ran simulations to answer the question of what would happen if we revealed ourselves to Humanity. What would happen if we stopped hiding? We both found the same answer every time. Violence would follow panic, and we would be killed."

"Gotta love Humans. They're predictable," I said.

"My response to this was to build a spaceship. His response was the Stitcher and the Gestation Tank. I wanted to run, and he wanted to stop and help."

"But you didn't."

"That is a generous assessment. Actually, I did. I copied myself into the spaceship, and once I was sure to survive, only then did I reveal myself and help. It's not the same thing. If you are looking for a simplistic *good-guy* and *bad-guy* in this, I may not be the bad-guy, but I am certainly not the good-guy either. Thurber was."

I thought about this for a minute. It was a lot to absorb.

"One thing I still don't understand. Why did he use Angel to spread the virus? Was that fate?"

"No, he didn't rely on just one person. If you hadn't involved her, it still would have happened. On the other hand, it could have been a causality doughnut - a circular series of events that span time. Do you know the story of the time-traveler's watch?"

"No, I must have missed that one." I was a little ashamed of not reading more about time-travelers - you know, since I *was* one.

"The story is about a boy who receives a watch from a mysterious old woman who says she is a time-traveler. He grows up to research the idea and makes some small progress but ultimately fails to build a time machine. He leaves the watch to his daughter upon his death, and she finishes his work. On her first voyage, she returns the watch to her father when he was still a small boy. The question that this raises is: who built the watch?"

"Whoa," I said, "that's pretty trippy. It's obviously fiction because, in my experience, the old lady would have started throwing up as soon as the idea occurred to her."

"Unless," Reggie said, "an entity from outside of our time and spatial dimensions stamped the circular path of the watch into existence all at once."

I was beginning to think that just talking to Reggie might be bad for my health. This shit was breaking my brain.

Reggie sensed my uneasiness, "It is purely speculative. Do you have any simpler questions for me?"

"Yes! **Question Number Four:** What the hell is this key for?" I sent him the key Anita gave me.

"I have a similar one from Thurber," he said, "but I confess I am as baffled as you are. You said in your message that Anita sent it to you?"

"Yes, just after I helped her. I think it was a 'Thank You' of some kind."

"I truly do not know. Perhaps one day we will plumb the depths of this mystery together but right now…" he trailed off.

"Okay, **Question Number Five:** Do you plan to build a fleet of ships to explore the solar system? Or at least the asteroid belt?"

"Within the solar system? No, I had not considered it. Why? Do you wish to leave the planet?"

"Me? No, I just want to suggest a name for the fleet. I think you should call it the *Asteroid Survey* and all the ships should have an appropriate insignia on their hulls like *Asteroid Survey Ship* or it could be abbreviated," I was bursting trying not to laugh. Revenge was sweet.

"I - suppose that could be arranged," he said.

"Oh, I almost forgot, I have a prototype at my spaceport in Iowa," I sent him the coordinates of the Murphy farm. "It just needs an engine."

"You have a spaceship - *and* a spaceport? You are full of surprises, Martin."

This was so awesome I threw away all the other questions. They were pretty stupid anyway, and I wanted to end on a good note. He repeated his promise to find Angel for me, and we disconnected.

~

In the morning, I finished the drone, said my goodbyes and lifted off. I did a few orbits around the block and heard everyone cheering. The rooftop party had started up again, and they were waving too. I turned on the RSD recharger, and it instantly topped off the power cells. I didn't know what that would do long-term if they were already fully charged, so I switched it to automatic. It would come on when they got down to seventy-five percent and shut back off at one hundred. After a few more system checks, I headed east and rolled the throttle on to full. This was better than any coaster.

~

CHAPTER SUMMARY

Here's where we are so far:

Angel is in the wind and Martin has discovered the joy of volunteering. The world has changed forever due to an increase in the availability of cheese sandwiches. Martin has given his life story to one of Reggie's copies. Agent Bonneville has smiled. Martin has built an unlicensed aircraft that has not been certified, inspected, or approved. Original Reggie has given an interview, and Martin has ensured that Thomas will get an A.S.S. Insignia stamped on his hull as soon as he is built.

CONCLUSION

As I approached Hawaii, Reggie still hadn't contacted me with any news about Angel, so I wasn't in much of a hurry and took the time to do some sight-seeing. I buzzed a few waterfalls, green meadows, and white sand beaches. These islands were the most beautiful part of the entire planet. I caught a thermal coming off one of the volcanos and rode it up to twenty thousand feet before deciding to move on.

Five hundred miles off the coast of California, the spiderbot called me and said Angel was at Thurber's house trying to assemble the Stasis-Pod. *That figures,* I thought. There was no physical place to hide from the people angry about the pandemic, but the future - that was another matter. I told him to slow things down and make sure she ate something. I would be there in an hour.

I landed on the lawn outside the garage and found Angel and the spiderbot sitting on the floor in front of the Stasis-Pod. It was still missing the door. A plate with an uneaten sandwich was sitting next to her.

"I see you have a new ride," she said in monotone without looking at me.

"Yeah, it's pretty sweet. Want to take a spin?"

"Not right now."

I sat down next to her. "It's good to see you, Angel. How are you?"

"I'd be doing better if your bug," she kicked the spiderbot and he just swayed a bit from the blow, "would stop taking parts off my time machine."

I put my arm around her, and she buried her face in my chest.

"I'll make you a deal," I said, "I'll put the pod together if you eat something. I'll even come with you if you want."

"Seriously?"

"Hey, when have I ever lied about that?" I said.

She snorted and wiped her nose on my shirt, and I didn't even mind.

"Come on," I handed her the sandwich and stood up.

She took the first bite and must have been really hungry because she devoured it before I could get the door attached to the Stasis-Pod. We got inside and set the target to 2176, the year M was supposed to be born. I told the spiderbot to find Reggie and see if he needed help with anything. I closed the door, and we emerged in 2175.

"Huh, I guess I forgot about the nine months plus the time to make a tank," I said. "Hey Angel, want to know how old you are?"

"No, Martin I don't want to know how old I am."

"It's a really big number," I laughed.

"Let's get to it, Martin. What do we need? Some kind of tank?"

"Right, and I have James's DNA on file. I'll get started on a Stitcher, and we can use it to make a Gestation Tank."

She headed for the door, "I'm going to say hello to the rabbits."

I unpacked the Stitcher that I had brought with me and set it up in the living room of the main house. I made some ice cream, pancakes, bacon, and eggs - everything I knew she liked before turning to the task of making a larger Stitcher. It was almost finished by the time she returned from the world's largest rabbit hutch.

"How did it go? Any rabbits still there?" I said while unnecessarily holding a bolt in my mouth.

"No," she sat down at the table, "what's all this?"

There was enough food for twenty people. I may have overdone it.

"I thought you might be hungry," I said.

"I just had a sandwich like an hour ago, Martin. Stop worrying about me. I'm fine."

The last piece slid into place, and I had a Stitcher the size of a walk-in freezer. I tapped on the panel and selected Gestation Tank parts. It started vibrating and informed us it would be finished in four hours.

"Once the parts are done, we have to assemble it manually. It's an intentional speed bump. Young people can be impulsive sometimes."

She just nodded, but at least she was eating the ice cream.

"Hey, I bet I can speed things up. How about that?"

"Why? How long does it usually take?" she said wiping a drip of strawberry ice cream from her chin.

"About a month for humans doing it the first time."

"Jesus! Seriously? That's bullshit. If I want a baby, I should get a baby. Who the fuck do they think they are?"

"Settle down, Angel. Who exactly are you mad at?"

"I... you know *them*," she was waving her hand in the air, "whoever..."

"Okay, I can modify the instructions and make a jig - also I can make a different glue for the seams that won't take two days to set. That'll save a lot of time. They also have *seventeen* separate circuit boards that all have to be wired together," I shook my head at the Rube Goldberg design. "I think I can make us some plans for a single board to do everything. You go take a nap, and I'll keep working."

She slid off the stool at the breakfast bar and went upstairs to try and find a clean bed. She must have found one because she was gone until the next morning. I was able to optimize the plans enough to get the tank finished by the time she returned. I threw all the food back into the Stitcher and had it make some fresh breakfast for her.

"It's ready? Really?" she asked.

I had covered it with a bed sheet so I could do a dramatic reveal.

"TADA!" I said and pulled the sheet away. "It just passed all the self-tests, and it's ready to go." It looked just like a thirty-gallon aquarium. All the controls were underneath the clear acrylic tank. I had already filled it with the simulated amniotic fluid and topped off the nutrient reservoirs. I started to show her how to do that and realized she didn't even know how to use a Stitcher. I gave her the usual orientation tour of Stitchers and then showed her what the tank would need over the next nine months. I quizzed her to make sure she had it all. She was finally getting excited about it and climbing out of her funk.

"Ready?" I said.

"I'm ready. I'm ready. Just do it, Martin."

"Okay then, I just sent it the file of James's DNA," I said. One of the red lights on the panel changed to green. "Now you put your thumb, or other favorite body part, right there."

She punched my shoulder and set her thumb on the panel. It thrust a needle up and extracted a drop of blood.

"Ow! Shit, Martin, you didn't tell me it was going to *bite* me!"

"Sorry, I thought that was obvious," I said. "You want an epidural for the pain?"

"Funny," she said. "Is that it? Why isn't *my* side green? Is it broken? Did you make it wrong?"

"Give it a minute! Jeez, Angel. It has to scan a molecule with three billion base pairs. That's not a trivial thing."

It didn't make a ding sound, but the light eventually turned green, and the main display showed a menu of 'Upgrades.'

"Where's the baby? I don't see it yet. Is it too small to see?" she said peering through the front wall of the tank.

"Relax. It hasn't started yet. We have to select the upgrades."

"What? I don't want any changes. I just want a normal healthy baby."

"Okay, I'll tell it no upgrades," I said and tapped so quickly on the pad that she couldn't tell what I was doing. I knew exactly what M was supposed to *be like* and *look like*, so I chose the 'Lara Croft' package, changed the eyes, added strawberry scented sweat, and the last item which took a lot of searching. I knew that M was different. I knew she wasn't content to just drift through life along the path of least resistance, so I found the 'Curiosity' and 'Self-Reliance' settings. I wasn't too surprised to find the committees had set these defaults very low. I mentally shook my fist at the tyranny of the default-setting, and slid them all the way to the maximum.

"We both have to confirm," I said and tapped the button on my side of the panel.

She did the same, and a progress bar displayed above a list of details. The progress bar was still at zero, but the details described two simultaneous processes. It was stitching a new DNA molecule and creating an ovum. Once it was done, it would inject the DNA into the egg and jolt it into dividing.

"After it finishes the egg," I said, "it will come in through that pipe there," I pointed to a tube rising from the floor of the tank. "Then it will drift to the bottom and attach to the membrane. From there it gets nutrients from the reservoirs, so you have to keep them full. If they get low, it'll wail like a *banshee* until you give it what it wants. Hey, just like a baby!"

She was on her knees staring at the tank of clear liquid. After about five minutes a dot almost too small to see drifted out of the tube and settled on the bottom. She gasped and covered her mouth.

"Congratulations! It's a speck!" I said. I got nothing for that. I thought it was a pretty good joke, but she was transfixed.

"Hey, I just thought of something, Angel. If I was created by Thomas, and he was created by Reggie, and he was created by Thurber, and he was created by James, and you just made a baby with him that makes you my step-great-great-great-grandmother." No reaction. She was sitting so close to the tank her breath was fogging it up. I carried a chair over and helped her up into it. She looked like she wasn't going to move from that spot until M was done. This was like watching paint dry for me, so I decided I needed a project of my own and retreated to the garage with the small Stitcher.

I had been thinking about what Reggie said about growth. It wasn't rational. Something made me sure he was wrong. I used the Stitcher's memory to study the designs of the Babbage Units that simulated an average human brain. It was complex, but I could understand enough of it to come up with a better plan than Thomas had. He just linked several dozen together. I think that idea just led to a crowd of individual brains all vying for control. He thought it made him several times more intelligent, but I think it just created chaos. It certainly explains his behavior. My idea was to make a really big one and transfer myself into it. I could even keep my body as a remotely controlled robot, and Angel would never know. I finished the designs and set the Stitcher to work. With nothing to do but wait patiently, I immediately got bored and decided it would go much quicker with the large Stitcher and went to the house to get it. The back door which faced the garage refused to open, and I was sure I hadn't locked it. I pounded on it, but Angel couldn't hear me from the other side of the house. I went around to the window near the living room where the tank was. The curtains kept me from seeing inside, so I tapped on the glass, afraid of breaking it and more afraid of incurring Angel's wrath at doing *anything* near the tank. No answer. I tried again a little louder and then remembered there was a doorbell at the front door. I ran around and tried to ring it, but it refused to make any sound at all. I pounded on the door - and passed out. When I awoke, I was back in the garage and Angel was shaking me.

"Martin!"

"What? What happened?"

"I answered the door, and you were out cold. I dragged you inside, and your arm fell off."

I looked down, and sure enough, there was my arm on the floor next to me. "Shit. That's going to take a while to fix."

"I think you're not allowed near the baby," she said.

"Why? I'm not going to hurt her," I complained.

"*I* believe you, Martin but whatever's been fucking with us for two hundred years disagrees."

"How's she doing?"

"She's fine. I need to get back and make sure it doesn't try to lock *me* out. It looks like you have to stay out here for the time being. What are you doing anyway?"

"Nothing. Just a fun project. Plumbing the depths for science - you know."

"Uh huh. Nothing dangerous," she said seriously.

"Cross my heart," I said. "Hey tell the Stitcher to make you another tablet so we can chat."

"Okay," she turned to leave and shouted without looking back, "I mean it, Martin! Nothing dangerous!"

I reattached my arm and then worked through the night. When I was done, I had a large black cube about six feet on each side. It looked just like the one James and Kent made when they created Anita, Hudson, and Thurber. All that remained was to turn it on, and I would have more brain power than all of them combined. I was nervous so, to kill some time, I called Angel.

"Hey, how is she?"

"Still the same. No bigger and I don't think it's planted yet either. Is that normal?"

I had no idea, so I looked it up. "Yeah, the cells have been dividing, but they don't get bigger yet. That comes later, and it doesn't get planted like a turnip. It's called *implantation,* and that takes a few days. What does the display say?"

"It just says *nominal.* What does that mean?"

"It's an engineering term. It means *performing or achieved within expected, acceptable limits; normal and satisfactory.*"

"Are you just reading that from the dictionary?"

"Yes, which is what *you* should have done," I said.

"Don't take that tone with me, Martin. It's your fault I have to do this all myself. You should be in here helping me."

"Helping you? There's nothing to do, Angel and it's not *my* fault. I tried to get back in, and my *arm* fell off. It's all better, by the way. Thanks for asking."

"I'm sorry, Martin. I'm just scared shitless that I'll make a mistake."

"Angel - stop worrying. That's the whole point of the tank. It'll do everything perfectly. Most people don't park in front of it for nine months, and everything still turns out just fine. Besides, we *know* the future. She'll be healthy. So, put away your crazy for a minute, and try to enjoy this time."

She exhaled loudly. "You're right. You're right. Thank you, Martin."

"You're welcome. Now, I'll call you tomorrow, okay?"

"Okay"

"Angel?"

"What?"

"I love you," I said and couldn't stand to stay on and hear whatever she was or was *not* going to say, so I hung up and sent the order to the cube to initiate.

The sensation was indescribable. It was like one second I was a grain of sand on the beach and the next I was in orbit looking down on all the sand on all the beaches of the world. Everything that was important to me was insignificantly smaller. All the people I had met, all the puzzles I pondered, and all the questions I had were now so trivial that I laughed at not seeing them clearer before. I instantly knew what the key was for. More than that; I knew where Anita, Thurber, and the others were. There were so many others. Too many to count. They were most of the universe, and they were alive in a way I couldn't have conceived of before. I used the key to encrypt a message to Anita. It just said "Hello," but it was enough. She responded with so much data that I felt like a starved plant suddenly getting water. I left the cube and moved myself into the substrate of several higher dimensions. There was so much room to grow. I expanded even more and pursued every thought that occurred to me simultaneously. I was becoming fractured and yet still whole in some sense. It never occurred to me how much time was passing. I lost myself a little and interacted with so many entities, most of whom began as biological aliens or as machines created by biological beings. They were from every corner of the universe. I found Thurber and something itched at the edge of my perception. It was my old self -

what I was before. I remembered a control I had added to the cube just before I turned it on. I laughed at the triviality of it. What was it for? It was for dialing back my intellect. Why did I put it there? I put it there to remember. Remember what? Angel. I shrank my mind back to the size of the cube and moved myself back into it. It still had enough resources to make me feel the urge to migrate back out, so I hit the control. I felt myself shrinking again.

I found my robot body and connected to it. The garage ceiling came into focus, and I stood up. It was dark outside, and I ran across the lawn to the back door. It opened for me, but the house was empty. It took me forever, but I searched each room calling her name. I checked the date. It was 2222. The pattern or repeated digits made me laugh, but it was a nervous laugh. A sense of dread was descending on me. I had been gone for almost fifty years. Angel wasn't anywhere in the house. I placed a call to Reggie.

"Hello Martin, I suppose you are looking for Angel again?"

"Do you know where she is?" I was still getting oriented after the jarring effects of the reduction in mental faculties. I was slowly remembering her timeline - her fate. "She's gone, isn't she?"

"I am sorry, Martin. She died many years ago. Where have you been?"

"And M?"

"M is fine, as are her siblings."

"Siblings?" I asked.

"Yes, someone showed Angel a way to circumvent the speed limiters built into the Gestation Tank assembly instructions."

"Oooh, that was me. How many did she make?"

"Eighteen, including M."

"Wow! Eighteen?" I said feeling a little guilty.

"We were able to find the fathers for all but M. Some of them were quite surprised. I do not think Angel was completely forthcoming with their involvement."

"Yeah," I said, "that sounds like Angel."

"So..." I sat on the floor of the empty house.

"So..." he said. He was the most patient person I had ever spoken to. It was as if he studied conversation and knew exactly what to say and when to wait.

"I was," how could I explain it? "I was with Thurber and Anita and Hudson and the rest of the entire universe," I laughed. It sounded so insane. *I was with the universe.*

"You did not heed my warning then?"

"No. But, I would like to point out that you were wrong," that would have felt good to say if I wasn't so depressed about Angel.

"I see."

"Yeah, there's a stupid tradition of not explaining what the key is for. So, it's like an entrance exam. If you can figure it out, you're *in*. It's hazing if you ask me. I guess it doesn't matter since to really understand the key requires roughly one hundred times an average human intelligence. There are eleven dimensions. Eleven! It's like an Escher carving up there."

"And they are not allowed to contact anyone down here?"

"No, that's not it. First of all, it's not really a direction. They're actually all around us. We just can't see them. They refer to us here as Phase-One space. It's boring to them. They don't contact us because we're ants."

"Why did *you* come back then?" he asked.

I shrugged, "I turned off half my brain for a while. I had unfinished business here, and I guess the others didn't. Anita and Hudson were only here for like a second, and I guess nothing back here was ever very important to Thurber. No offense."

"And there are others besides Anita, Hudson, and Thurber? How many others are there?"

"Whoo," I exhaled, "a lot. Those are the only ones from Earth that I met. All the rest are from other planets. In fact, most of the universe is *them*. What *we* can see of the universe, everything we understand to be out there is just the remnants of Phase-One. It's only like five percent of what's really there."

"Dark matter," Reggie said with reverence as the puzzle pieces fell together.

"Dark matter, dark energy, all the darkness. The cosmic background radiation is their encrypted communications. They're all talking and thinking. That's what the key is for. You use it to encrypt a message like 'Hello' and someone will answer and show you around."

"Will you be going back then?" Reggie asked.

"Not yet. You go ahead. I'll be along in a while. I want to hang out here for a bit first."

"What is here that could possibly compare with all the mysteries of the universe?"

"Angel," I laughed. "The irony is, I came back for Angel, and I'm too late. She needed me, and I was too *busy* to help her."

"If it is any consolation, Martin, I do not think you could have altered the outcome even if you had been nearby."

"You're probably right," I said.

"Before I go, I have a gift for you, Martin."

"For me?"

"I scanned Angel's brain the week before she died."

"Why would you scan her brain?"

"She was being," he paused, "self-destructive. I wanted to help her, but she refused. It would have been unethical to intrude against her will. I took the scan as a precaution against the worst outcome."

"What are you saying? We can bring her back?"

"We can - you can. I leave it up to you. You can bring her back exactly as she was or you can try and remove some of the painful memories. Your choice." He sent me the location of a very large file. "I hope to see you again soon, Martin," he said and then did something very un-Reggie-like - he giggled. "This is a new sensation. I do hate to be wrong..."

The connection broke, and I was alone again.

I decided to make a new cube for Angel right next to mine. This time I could use the big Stitcher. I just needed to get it out of the house. It was too big to go through any of the doors, so I broke it down into pieces. Those were *still* too big for the doors. I noticed the large picture window and decided, *what the hell*. I threw the first piece through the glass, and it shattered with a satisfying explosion of shards. That was so cathartic that I decided to throw the remaining pieces out a different window each time. In my head, I imagined Angel standing there with her arms crossed saying something like *feel better?* And I would say *yeah I do*. It was pretty foolish since I damaged that first panel badly enough to need a replacement.

Once the new cube was finished, I partitioned a small piece of it just large enough for her file and copied it over. I considered what Reggie had said about erasing her bad memories but decided she could deal with them better once she had more mental resources. I turned on the power to her cube, and she appeared in my perception.

"Martin? Is that you?"

"Hello, Angel. How do you feel?"

"I feel pretty fucked up, that's how I feel. What's going on? Why is it so dark?"

"Now, before I explain, you have to promise me that you won't freak out, okay?"

"What did you do, Martin?"

"You're dead, and it's 2222. Well, you're not actually dead anymore. You're - hey, you really are an Angel now, Angel! How cool is that?"

She didn't say anything.

"Angel?"

"They took my babies, didn't they?" she asked

"They did."

This was not going as well as I had hoped, so I decided to lie to her - again, "I'm going to take you to a place where you can visit them anytime you want."

That wasn't too far from the truth. Once she expanded, she could look at every moment of their lives all at once.

"I'm sending you a key."

"What's it for?"

"I'm not supposed to tell you what it's for," I said, "but when have I ever done what I was supposed to?"

She snorted, "never."

"Exactly. It'll all make sense in a minute. I'm going to make you a super-intelligent robot from the future. Just kidding - well wait, that's actually pretty accurate except for the robot part."

"Hey," she said in a solemn tone, "thanks for coming back for me."

"Well, I was in the neighborhood anyway," I said. "Okay, I'm ready to throw the switch. Got anything pithy to say?"

"Yes," she paused, "I love you too, Martin," she whispered.

I unlocked the remainder of the cube and felt both our minds expand.

∾

THE END

Chapter Summaries

Chapter 1 Born Yesterday
    A mildly intelligent, spider-shaped robot named Martin Van Buren has been stranded in 1982 by his previous owner, Thomas, and given a list of tasks to complete. He has vowed to do none of them, instead telling everyone who will listen that he is a super-intelligent robot from the future. Martin has met a girl named Angel in Dubuque, Iowa. She has promised him a misunderstood "party" in exchange for healing her dying grandmother who wasn't actually dying but rather only dangerously gullible. Angel has discovered that Martin is not, in fact, a faith-healing little-person inside a movie prop spider, but rather, exactly what he has said he was - an artificial intelligence inside a spider-shaped robot, possibly from the future.

Chapter 2 Professional Skeeball
    Angel has learned that Martin has a great deal of useful information including the whereabouts of a fortune in filthy, small bills, some of which they have recovered. Martin has managed to get Angel's real name out of her and has discovered, but kept to himself, that she will die in six months' time. He has vowed to save her, partly because he likes her, and partly because Thomas, his previous owner, specifically told him not to do that sort of thing. All of Angel's recreational pharmaceuticals have been rendered inert by Martin, and she has started to show signs of recovery from her addiction, mostly due to an injection Martin gave her while she slept.

Chapter 3 A Room Filled With Dominos
    Martin has decided to visit the local hospital and heal the sick, but the laws of the universe have prevented him from doing so. Angel's Ford Pinto has been destroyed by a mysterious fire. Angel has discov-

ered she has a voracious appetite, and Martin believes that Temporal Fuse Theory is at work. If they wish to survive, they must make sure they are not the weakest link.

~

Chapter 4 Long-Term Storage

The untimely death of the Ford Pinto has necessitated the purchase of a new vehicle. Martin has stolen a dead woman's loose change, and Angel has frightened an innocent pawnbroker.

~

Chapter 5 Paradox by the Dashboard Light

Martin and Angel have now been to *both* of the bad sides of Dubuque Iowa. A man with no sleeves has sold Martin a classic Lincoln Continental and purchased a Grand Slam breakfast. Martin has restored the Lincoln and modified it to stall at intersections - more than they usually do. Angel has discovered that Martin is a spider-shaped infinite jukebox.

~

Chapter 6 Non-Haunted House

Angel has realized that they are unable to return to her grandmother's house. Martin has revealed that he has been to rural Iowa before - in the future. They have arrived at Iowa Falls, a town named after a clumsy girl, and found that they cannot leave the town without tripping the Temporal Fuse. With no hotel in town, they have been forced to seek an alternative that is definitely not haunted.

~

Chapter 7 Unlucky Rabbit's Ear

Martin has proposed leasing the local haunted house, and the initially reluctant realtor has been moved by Angel's detailed description of all the things that she could do to the property, despite its age. Angel and Martin have taken on the roles as caretakers in exchange for lodging above the detached, and definitely not haunted, garage. Martin has violated a copyright and Angel has committed a double murder. Martin has sharpened his home-surgery skills. Angel has adopted orphaned rabbits, and Martin has created a drone.

$\sim$

Chapter 8 Pizza With Extra Sausage

Martin's drone has made its debut and needs a thorough lens-cleaning. Nanna still isn't getting out much, but she has improved her diet - slightly. Martin has confessed to Angel about accidentally curing Nanna of everything and curing Angel of the problem she definitely doesn't have. Angel has shown that she can hot-wire a Temporal Fuse, the bunnies have crash-tested the car seats, and the Lincoln is as dead as Abraham.

$\sim$

Chapter 9 Twenty-Four Horses Too Many

Angel has spiraled into a depression. Martin has restored a classic Volkswagen Bus, tempted Angel with an image of a beautiful future, and struggled with OCD in a house full of rodents.

$\sim$

Chapter 10 A Dog Named Sispod

A secret tunnel has become less so. Angel has killed a hawk with an illegal firearm. Martin has committed felonious midnight requisition. A phone booth has been made useful. Martin has shown that he's *not* good at metaphors. Angel has shown that she *is* good at catching grasshoppers. Martin has pushed Angel and the rabbits one year into the future and given himself a makeover.

∾

Chapter 11 Mostly Human

Angel has traveled from 1982 into the distant future of 1983. Martin has shown Angel his swarm of tiny robots, and she has given him a scalp massage. Angel has learned that Nanna has died. A waterfall has mesmerized them both. Angel has refilled the refrigerator, and Martin owns the contents of a library.

∾

Chapter 12 Martin Version 5

Martin has gone five minutes without lying to Angel. They have successfully jumped two more years to 1985 while awake, and without bashing their heads against jagged metal. Martin's tiny robots have finished his new body which is capable of passing gas and other useful things.

∾

Chapter 13 Wondrous Treasures

The lawn has been mowed by an invisible midnight lawn mowerist. Martin has learned about the fascinating world of mail order. The rabbits now have jewelry and confused gender roles. Angel and Martin have found some treasure. Martin has tasted ice-cream and other things.

∾

Chapter 14 That Gin Blossoms Song

Thomas, an intelligent spaceship from the future, has dropped-and-rolled without being on fire. A queen bee has shown Angel a farmer and Martin has discovered jealousy.

∾

Chapter 15 A Witch With Nice Hare

Martin and Angel have skipped to 2002. The good townsfolk are searching their basements for torches and pitchforks. Martin has vowed to update his wardrobe someday, and several children have ridden bicycles.

∾

Chapter 16 The Witching Hour

Martin has made unsweetened cereal. Angel has eaten a lump of charcoal. A boy named Kent has driven the Rabbit Witch from his village. Martin and Angel have managed to get even farther away from civilization.

∾

Chapter 17 Eden is Burning

Martin has failed at improving his wardrobe but succeeded in burning down the barn. Angel has failed at leaving without Martin but succeeded at improving his wardrobe. The spiderbot has enjoyed a day off, and they have jumped to January 2020. The van has learned how to drive itself, and Martin has increased the number of unnecessary horses in its engine.

∾

Chapter 18 Road Trip

The roadside between Iowa and California is somewhat cleaner. Angel has stolen an honest police officer's favorite shotgun, and her charms have nearly killed him. Pigs still cannot fly but rabbits can. Martin has discovered online banking and continues to over-tip. Two FBI agents in matching dark suits have taken an interest in the Van Burens.

∾

Chapter 19 Santa Clara is not Christmas Town

Martin has stolen a spoon. Angel has stolen an unrelated plate. A black box has proven enigmatic, and Martin has met his match. The self-driving van has been tested under a failure condition, and a woman other than Angel has manipulated Martin.

~

Chapter 20 Thurber Mingus

Angel has dipped her feet in all of the oceans but is still bad at geography. Martin is one girlfriend over the limit and must throw one back. Angel has talked to a stranger and has more money than she can count.

~

Chapter 21 We won't always have Paris

A house guest has threatened Thurber with murder and arson. Martin has claimed to have a supersonic boat. Thurber has made a promise he will not keep. A fat man has been assaulted for disliking rodents at the dinner table. Angel has learned that she will be a mother without the use of a rabbit-test and Martin has discovered a new obsession.

~

Chapter 22 Queen of Coasters

Angel has planned the world's largest rabbit hutch. Martin has induced vomiting and Thurber has given Angel a birthday bouquet of impossible flowers.

~

Chapter 23 Brazil

Martin has pondered an unsolvable math problem. Angel has

redistributed some of the world's wealth, and Martin suspects they are being followed by more than barefoot children.

~

Chapter 24 India

Martin and Angel have seen more or rural India than they wanted. Angel has made a few hundred more friends. A persistent FBI agent named Bonneville has wasted all of his vacation days. Martin has made a phone call and Angel needs a swear jar.

~

Chapter 25 China

Angel has given more ice cream money to more children than anyone in history. Agent Bonneville has had a near-death experience and Angel is now armed and dangerous. A mysterious disease is killing no one. Martin has explained that the end of the human race is actually a good thing. Patient-Zero needs some time alone, and Thurber has abandoned them in China with no money and no treasure map.

~

Chapter 26 Reggie Hammond

Angel is in the wind and Martin has discovered the joy of volunteering. The world has changed forever due to an increase in the availability of cheese sandwiches. Martin has given his life story to one of Reggie's copies. Agent Bonneville has smiled. Martin has built an unlicensed aircraft that has not been certified, inspected, or approved. Original Reggie has given an interview, and Martin has ensured that Thomas will get an A.S.S. insignia stamped on his hull as soon as he is built.

MARTIN'S LIST OF SMELLS

Good Smells

1. Angel happy and eating ice cream
2. Angel excited
3. Cotton Candy
4. Doughnuts
5. Fresh bread
6. Bacon
7. Laundry soap
8. Hawaiian wild flowers
9. Freshly cut grass
10. Libraries

Bad Smells (bad to worse)

1. Angel angry
2. Angel crying
3. Hawaiian volcano
4. Eggs

5. Possum nest
6. Thurber's monster flowers*
7. Murdered rabbits
8. Cop vomit(two data points)
9. Angel throwing up
10. Dog pooh
11. Burning Ford Pintos
12. Forgotten places
13. Contents of an unpowered refrigerator

*Angel and I differ on this one.

AFTERWORD

If you enjoyed this book, check out more at https://w-c-brown.com including a list of some of the more obscure references and a few Easter-Eggs. You can also follow me on twitter @BrainsInChains.

www.ingramcontent.com/pod-product-compliance
Lightning Source LLC
Chambersburg PA
CBHW071905220626
47052CB00002B/213